The Trail Boss

STAND-ALONE NOVEL

A Western Historical Adventure Book

by

Zachary McCrae

CW01425538

Disclaimer & Copyright

Table of Contents

Letter from Zachary McCrae

I'm a man who loves plain things; a cup of strong coffee in the morning, a good book at noon and his wife's embrace at night. I want to write stories that take you from the hand and show you what it meant to be someone who tried to make ends meet and find their own way in 19-century United States. I've been this someone for a long time in my life, always looking for my next gig after my parents' sudden death, always finding new friends but somehow not being able to stick with 'em. It's easy to find quantity in your life but what about quality?

At the age of 50, and after my baby boy, Jeb, and my sweet daughter, Janette, went away to study East, with my sweet wife, Mrs. Maryanne Mc Crae, we moved back to my home town and my dad's ranch close to the Rockies. After a series of health issues that have brought me even closer to our Lord, I've officially started writing those stories I always loved to read. I'm tending my land and animals now with the help of Maryanne, and I'm grateful for each day I get to walk on this world we call earth. As the saying goes, "Nature gave us all something to fall back on, and sooner or later we all land flat on it," so I want to take care of it just the way it has taken care of my dad and mom, and my cousins.

My adventure stories are my legacy to my children and to all of the readers that will honor me by following my work. God bless you and your families and our land! Thank you.

Stay safe but adventurous,

Zachary McCrae

Prologue

15 miles south of the Washita River

October 1875

Paul sat far from the campfire, the rifle across his lap gleaming in the fading light as he ran a cloth over the barrel. The deep tan of his skin blended with the hides he wore, making him look more like part of the land than the man leading the trail. Broad shoulders hunched forward, he moved the cloth with slow precision.

Rocco and Jody, the two hands traveling with him, murmured in the distance; their voices drifted over, but the night had brought its own kind of quiet—one Paul had learned to respect.

A branch snapped behind him. His fingers stilled.

Suddenly, Rocco's laughter cut through the night like gravel over stone, his broad frame casting a long shadow in the light. "Jody, you 'member the time you near drowned in that creek outside of Wichita?"

Jody sat with his knees drawn up, poking at the fire with a stick, his wiry form restless even at rest. He never seemed to settle, thin arms constantly in motion, as though he had too much energy for his body to contain.

"I wasn't drownin', just... takin' my time gettin' out. Water was cold as death, though."

As the two close friends talked, Paul aimed his rifle's barrel into the darkness. Its weight felt solid against his palm.

The ease between his two companions stirred unpleasantness in his chest, leading his mind to memories best forgotten. They were like brothers, their bond forged through shared years, jokes, and experiences on the trail.

Paul turned his eyes back to the darkness, but the knot in his chest tightened. He tried to think of the last time he'd felt that kind of connection. Not since—

No. I won't think about that.

He shook the thought off as another crunch sounded in the brush, closer this time.

"Your face was blue enough, might as well've been drownin'!"

"Shut up." Jody's reddish hair stuck out in wild tufts beneath his battered hat, and his freckled face remained constantly coated in a fine layer of dust, no matter how often he wiped it away. "Paul's probably tryin' to sleep."

Paul eased the hammer back on his rifle, scanning the dark tree line. The scent of damp earth mingled with the faint smoke from the fire, but underneath it, something else stirred. Fear. Desperation.

Two men stepped out of the trees, ragged clothes hanging from their gaunt frames, guns drawn and pointed at Jody and Rocco.

Jody scrabbled backward. "What—"

Paul fired before anyone else had a chance to react. The crack echoed through the night as the first man's head snapped forward, his body crumpling into the dirt.

Rocco jumped to his feet, knocking over his tin cup. "Holy—"

The second man gaped, his eyes wide, then turned and ran.

Paul stood and made his way to the fallen body, nudging it with his boot. "Ain't nothin' to it." He shrugged. "Man's just desperate."

Rocco wiped his face with his sleeve, his hand shaking slightly. "You think he'll come back?"

"No. Man like that's runnin' for good."

Paul crouched beside the dead man, pulling a torn map from his pocket and tossing it toward the fire.

Jody let out a breath. "Damn. Thought we were goners."

"You were too busy jawin' to notice what's around you." Paul shook his head and sat next to them. The night pressed close again, but it felt a little quieter now.

Rocco crouched down to pick up his cup; when he spoke, his voice was a little smaller than before. "Paul… you reckon the trail's gettin' worse?"

Paul scratched his chin through his beard. "Maybe."

Jody shuddered. "Railway's puttin' us outta business. Ain't much left for cattle herders."

"World's changin'. Don't care what we think," Paul said.

"Railway or no railway," Rocco muttered, pulling his blanket closer. "Damn shame. Used to be you could walk these trails without worryin' someone was gonna take a shot at you."

Paul glanced at the sky, where the first stars were blinking into view. The fire crackled and popped, but didn't do much to ease the chill settling in his bones. The time of the trail was coming to an end, as sure as the sun rose in the morning.

I'll have to go home. Ice filled his gut at the thought.

"It's the way things go," he muttered. "Rail's comin', whether we like it or not."

Jody tossed another stick into the fire. "And what happens after that, huh? No more trails, no more cattle drives... What's a man supposed to do?"

Laying back, Rocco took off his Stetson and stretched out, folding his muscular arms behind his head. "Maybe it's for the best. Ain't much of a life out here, nohow."

Rocco looked more at ease under the stars than most men would be in their own beds. His hat had plastered his grizzled hair to his skull, exposing the lines etched into his sun-beaten face to the dim firelight. Those wrinkles told the story of a man who'd lived his life hard and fast.

Looking away, Paul tightened his jaw. "Some folks ain't got a choice."

The fire crackled as the night deepened, stretching lengthening shadows across the camp. Jody rolled over in his bedroll, muttering something under his breath. Rocco yawned, eyes already drifting closed.

Paul remained where he was, his back against a cold rock. He didn't bother trying to sleep. Otherwise, the dreams would come.

Chapter One

Washita River

The air hung thick with moisture, and the steady roar of the Washita River pounded in Elsie's ears. The cattle moved nervously, their hooves churning up mud. There was no sign of a ferry this time, like there'd been at the Brazos. The short curls of her hair stuck to her forehead beneath the brim of her hat as her chest tightened at the speed of the current.

It didn't matter.

She *had* to cross it.

"Keep 'em movin'." Her worn wool shirt stuck to her skin, her too-new leather chaps creaking as her legs squeezed tighter around the horse's sides.

She snapped the reins, and her horse stepped forward, closer to the riverbank. She tugged at the worn brim of her hat, a Stetson that had seen too many rains and too few dry patches, and tightened the bandana around her neck. Both the hat and the bandana served to hide the sharp line of her jaw and the feminine curve of the cupid's bow on her small mouth. She prayed no one would notice that her frame was too slender even for a scrawny young man.

You're Eli, *not* Elsie. *You're not a woman here.*

The river spray mingled with dust, leaving a muddy smell she'd come to know well on the trail. Marcus, standing on the other side of the herd, pulled a lariat out of his saddle, coaxing the cattle with low, calming whistles. He rubbed the gray stubble on his chin, his hat casting faint shadows over his weathered face.

"Ain't no use rushin', Eli," he called, his voice like the rumble of distant thunder. He stooped to pick up a handful of dirt, crumbling it between his fingers. "River don't care about time. Just weight."

Marcus's one good eye flickered toward Elsie's face, lingering for a split second longer than usual. He looked like he wanted to say something more, but he didn't.

Her stomach tightened. Had he figured out her secret?

No, that's impossible. Just focus on the cattle.

"Ain't time for lingerin'," she said. "Cattle'll spook if we dawdle."

Water lapped at her horse's hooves, and her breath caught. She tightened her grip on the reins.

"Come on now," she muttered. "It's just water, not a damn cliff."

Her horse stepped closer to the riverbank until the muddy water was churning just below her. Elsie swallowed hard, her pulse quickening. She couldn't swim. She'd never learned, and now the Washita seemed ready to swallow her whole.

Shaking herself, she straightened her shoulders. *Eli isn't afraid of a river.*

"Just keep 'em steady." Marcus pushed through the herd, giving a soft click of his tongue and wiping the sweat from his brow as he passed. "The river don't bite."

Elsie pulled her hat down, as if it could shield her from the relentless pull of the water. Her hands shook, but she pressed her heels into her horse's sides. Why couldn't it stop being so jittery?

The metal of her spurs clinked against the stirrups, the leather reins stiff in her hands from long hours of riding.

"Keep your damn head straight," she muttered to herself, louder this time.

The horse's hooves sank into the muddy bank as she kicked it into the river. The water rose above her boots. She swallowed again as the cold grip of the current crawled up her spine, and her horse snorted and tried to turn around.

"Hell's bells," she whispered, snapping the reins again.

A sharp whistle cut through the air as he urged a wayward cow back into the herd and approached the edge of the water, years of experience showing in every deliberate step. His bad eye, clouded and milky, remained still, but the other flicked to Elsie.

"You push 'em any faster, they'll scatter. Ain't worth drownin' over."

Eli isn't afraid of drowning.

"Don't need you ridin' me, Marcus. I know my damn job."

The words came out harsher than she meant, but the water—pulling harder now—made it difficult to think straight. She could feel the horse's muscles twitching. Trying to find steady ground, she shifted her weight, but the thrice-damned horse wouldn't stop fighting her. The leather of her McClellan saddle creaked beneath her, its worn pommel slick with moisture.

Marcus's gaze rested on her for longer than she'd like before he tipped his hat and responded. "Ain't sayin' that. Just don't want the river to take you."

There was something soft in his tone—concern, maybe?

Elsie gritted her teeth and urged her horse onward, her breath catching as the ground beneath her shifted. The current pulled harder, and water surged against her legs.

"Come on, keep goin'," she muttered through clenched teeth.

Her horse stumbled.

They both went under.

Elsie's lungs burned as the cold grip of the river swallowed her whole. She caught a glimpse of Marcus standing by the riverbank, his shout drowned by the rush of the current. His arms waved, but he wasn't moving fast enough.

Just before the water swallowed her whole, Elsie heard him call out, "Paul, help!"

The current tore at her limbs, and her chest tightened with each passing second as she kicked and tried to get out. Her vision blurred. The world around her faded to a churning mass of gray and blue.

Help me!

Hands—strong and steady—clamped around her arms, dragging her free of the water's relentless grasp.

Her head broke the surface with a gasp, her chest heaving as air flooded her lungs. She coughed violently, feeling the river's chill seep deeper into her bones. A rough voice cut through the haze of water and panic.

"Don't let go."

Elsie shivered uncontrollably as she was hauled out of the water. Her lean body trembled from the cold, and her soaked clothes clung tightly to her frame. It would be harder to keep up the illusion of being a man if anyone examined her now-visible curves. She tried to ignore how her chest heaved with each ragged breath and pulled her sodden hat lower.

A muscled arm wrapped tightly around her waist, hauling her onto the back of a horse. She felt the warmth of a man's body against her as he settled her in front of him. Her hands slipped on the slick leather of the saddle.

She heard Marcus's voice close by. "Got him?"

Warm breath tickled Elsie's ear as the man who'd saved her replied, "He's fine."

She blinked, water dripping from her lashes, and craned her neck to look up into the face of her rescuer. Recognition flickered—this had to be the trail boss. Aldo had mentioned him in passing, but she hadn't thought they'd meet like this. A Colt revolver hung low at his hip, and his boots, caked in mud, bore the scuffs of countless miles.

His beard, brown with some early flecks of gray, gave him a distinguished air, as if he'd already seen and done more than most men his age. Beneath the wide-brimmed hat, his eyes held the sharpness of a man who missed little, the creases around them deepening as he weighed the risks. Those dark eyes met hers, serious and intense, as if they saw through the disguise she wore.

Don't think about that. Eli doesn't worry.

The man was as tall and broad as an ox with a thick beard framing his face. He ran a hand over his cropped hair, the short strands barely moving under his palm. The wet leather of his jacket clung to the thick muscles beneath, the hides he wore making him look like part of the wilderness itself.

"Eli Wadsworth?"

The name felt foreign to her, but she forced herself to nod, her throat too raw to speak. The weight of the man's gaze lingered, and for a brief, breathless second, she worried that his hands—so close—would feel the truth hidden beneath her soaked clothes.

"Aldo told me what ya look like." The man grunted, and his grip tightened around her as the horse splashed toward the riverbank. "What'd you reckon, crossin' here?"

Elsie stiffened. She'd just had a little accident; that didn't mean she'd chosen the wrong place to cross! She shifted, trying to sit up straighter, her soaked boots slipping against the horse's flanks.

"Cattle..." She coughed as the words scraped her throat. "Cattle needed movin'."

"Damn near lost the whole herd." His eyes flicked briefly to the river before settling on her, his grip still firm around her. "And yourself."

"Ain't the first scrape I've been in." She clenched her fists and glanced toward the herd, which was still trying to escape the water's edge.

Alright... Maybe this wasn't the best place after all...

"I saw drownin'."

"I had it handled."

He snorted and pulled the horse to a stop on firmer ground. He swung down in one fluid motion, his boots hitting the mud with a dull thud. He reached up, gripping her waist again and pulling her down.

Elsie stumbled, her legs still shaky from the river's pull, but she steadied herself, wiping a wet strand of hair from her face and tucking it back under her Stetson.

"I don't know what you think you're tryin' to prove, but drownin' sure ain't gonna do it." His voice softened, just a bit, but the edge remained.

"Don't need you leadin' me over no river," Elsie grumbled.

"You might not need it, but you'll get it all the same." He loomed over her. "Next time, listen."

A chill wind whipped through the clearing, cutting straight through her wet clothes. Her lips parted, but no words came. Instead, she dropped her gaze to the ground, teeth gritted.

"Get yourself dried off." He sighed, taking a step back. "We've still got a long way ahead of us."

Elsie nodded stiffly, her fingers fumbling with the straps of her saddle. Her heart hammered in her chest, not just from the river's pull but from something about the way his gaze had held her—a weight she couldn't quite shake.

Enough. Eli doesn't care about how anyone looks at him.

Her wounded pride felt heavier than the cold water dripping from her hair and clothing. The man had already turned toward the cattle, barking orders to the rest of the hands as he tugged his horse toward the herd.

He didn't even ask if I'm alright.

"Hell of a way to treat someone you just pulled outta the river," she muttered.

"Hell of a way to get yourself killed," he shot back, snatching a rope from his saddle and tossing it to one of the men. "Worse, you damn near dragged the whole herd under with you. Ain't no sense in it."

Elsie ground her teeth as fire rise in her chest. "Didn't have a choice, not with that storm rollin' in—or do you not see it comin'?"

"Always got a choice." The man kept his focus on the cattle, pulling his gloves off with sharp jerks and wiping his hands on his pants. "You picked the wrong one."

Elsie clenched her fists at her sides, his words digging under her skin like thorns. "I made the best call I could, considerin' the river was risin' and spookin' the herd."

The man turned, his dark eyes locking onto hers, though he hadn't moved any closer. His horse shifted uneasily beside him, hooves sinking into the wet ground. His saddle was well-worn but solid, the silver conchos gleaming in the faint light. The stirrups hung low, adjusted to fit his long frame, and the rawhide reins in his hands looked as though they'd seen more years than most men.

"The herd was spookin' 'cause you kept tryin' to drown 'em."

"I made the call I thought was right," she said. "You got a problem with it, take it up with Aldo."

He stared at her for a long moment, the silence between them heavy as the wind picked up, whipping her wet clothes against her skin. He finally shook his head, turning back toward the horses.

"Oh, we will." He pulled himself into the saddle with one smooth motion. "But don't settle in. We ain't stoppin' yet."

Elsie's hands trembled, though whether from cold or anger, she couldn't tell.

Stay calm. Eli is supposed to be more in control of this.

"Ain't no need to remind me." She kicked at the mud as she watched him ride off. Her heart raced as frustration bubbled up in her chest. She took a shaky breath, then called out, louder this time. "What's your name, anyhow?"

He stopped, turning in the saddle. His eyes met hers across the distance.

"Paul."

There was something unreadable in his tone, something that made her feel like he saw more than she wanted him to. Elsie stared after him, her heart still galloping. She couldn't shake the feeling that he was waiting for her to slip up, and she hated it.

Marcus approached and gave her a once-over. "You alright?"

"Ain't nothin' I can't handle."

He studied her for a moment longer before turning back toward the herd. "We still got a ways to go," he murmured, his fingers brushing the brim of his hat as he walked off.

The horse and cattle hooves slapped against the wet ground, filling the silence between Elsie and Marcus as they rode beside each other. Her small mouth tightened, and she bit back a curse as she felt the familiar pressure against her cupid's bow—a sing of femininity the men teased 'the young trailhand' for. The herd, formerly restless from the river crossing, had settled, merging with Paul's group into a noisy, shifting mass.

Marcus glanced sideways, his weathered face calm under the brim of his hat. "You handled it well back there."

"Didn't feel that way,"

He straightened, his fingers brushing the reins as he chuckled. "Paul's got a way with words, no doubt—but he pulled you out, didn't he?"

"Didn't ask for savin'." She let out a short laugh, bitter and sharp, and tugged her hat lower over her forehead, shielding her face from the drizzle that had begun to fall. "Could've made it on my own."

"Maybe. But the trail's got a way of showin' folks they ain't as invincible as they think."

"I'm fine."

Eli can pull his weight.

"Still, don't mean you gotta carry it alone."

Elsie shifted in her saddle, the ache of the day's ride settling into her bones. "Ain't got a choice."

Ahead, Paul slowed his horse, scanning the horizon before nudging the herd onward. She couldn't shake the way he'd looked at her earlier—like he saw right through her. Not just *Eli* or *Elsie*, but something deeper, something she hadn't noticed herself.

Marcus gave her a long look, his face softening just a bit. "Maybe not. But you've still got miles to go, Eli. Don't let pride be the thing that trips you."

Elsie bit back a retort, the slap of hooves and lowing of cattle filling the space where her words would've landed. *Pride.* Maybe that was part of it, but there was more.

There always was.

The wet ground sucked at the cattle's hooves, and Elsie knew they'd have to camp soon. The thought of facing Paul again, after everything, made her stomach twist.

ZACHARY MCCRAE

Chapter Two

10 miles north of the Washita River

Paul stood with his back against a gnarled cottonwood, arms crossed, his eyes tracing Eli's movements by the fire. The kid stirred the kindling too slowly, too hesitantly for a man who'd claimed to know the trail. The flames flickered weakly, and Paul couldn't help but wonder how someone like Eli ended up here.

No hardened hand fumbles with fire like that.

Eli's features were too soft for most men Paul knew too. Short, dark hair curled under the brim of Eli's hat, messy, but clean. The kind of hair that looked like it should be longer. His skin had the telltale tan of someone used to being outdoors, but his frame was lean, smaller than most trail hands Paul had worked with.

Not the kind of body that's been worn by ranch work.

"That how you work? Slow as molasses?"

Eli's fingers stilled over the kindling, gripping the stick tightly before tossing it into the flames. "Fire'll catch when it's ready. Rushin' don't change a thing."

Paul had come up from nothing himself, working his way from scout to trail master after years of hard riding and bloody knuckles. He'd earned his place through grit and instinct, keeping men alive across a thousand miles of bad land. That wasn't luck—it was survival.

"Out here, slow's a good way to die. You learn that, you stay alive."

He stepped forward and squatted by the fire as dusk settled over the camp. The restless herd quieted as the evening stretched out. Paul's examined Eli's face, searching for a crack in that guarded expression.

Why do you look like you don't belong?

"I'm still here, ain't I?" Eli prodded the fire with long, slender fingers.

Paul was squinting at the fire when Marcus passed by, casting a glance over Eli that lingered just a moment too long.

Paul caught Marcus's eye for a second before the older man looked away, scratching at the stubble on his chin.

What was that about?

Paul looked back at Eli. "Nearly went under in the Washita."

For all his calm now, Eli had thrashed in those waters like a man who'd never faced nature's wrath before.

Near them, Rocco cackled with a mouth full of jerky at something Jody had said. Rocco had been running his mouth since they made camp, always full of words but never work. Oh, he did his share of chores, but grudgingly, and rarely offered to help anyone except Jody with theirs.

Eli sighed, and the cupid's bow on his small mouth creased. "Made a bad call."

"You risked cattle—and your hide." Paul shook his head. "Shouldn't gamble on neither."

"My mistake, my consequence."

Paul raised his eyebrows. Most men didn't admit mistakes so easy, and those that did were usually hiding something else. The way Eli fidgeted, it was like the kid was bracing for a hit that didn't come.

"Aldo said you knew your way 'round the trail." Paul's eyes flicked to the herd, then back. "I don't see it."

Though, to be fair, I don't know much about Aldo either.

He'd seen Aldo's name in the papers nearly two months ago—a last call for anyone crazy enough to risk the trail one more time before these cattle drives became just another memory of the past. A heading north, to Kansas, driving close to two hundred head of longhorns up the Chisholm Trail, bound for the railheads in Wichita.

Paul didn't trust Aldo much, and considering that Eli was acting like he didn't know only one of them was getting paid, his instinct seemed to have been right.

However, Paul needed the money, so he took what work he could get. After losing his father, his ranch had crumbled, and when... *she*'d left, what little reason he'd had to stay in Texas had dissolved.

Trail driving had become his last refuge.

After a moment, Eli shrugged. "Aldo ain't wrong."

"Maybe," Paul said, watching him through the haze of the firelight, "but words don't mean much. Gotta see for myself."

"Ain't lookin' for anyone's approval out here."

Paul smirked, but didn't respond.

Rocco stood up and wandered a few paces off, muttering something about adding greens to the stew.

I'm surprised he's even bothering.

"Hell, this looks good enough to eat!" Rocco bent down, fingers reaching toward the stems of a plant, about to pluck it.

"Not that one!" Eli crossed the short distance quickly. "Touch that, and you'll be dead 'fore dawn."

Rocco froze, his hand hovering in the air. "What?"

Eli knelt, brushing aside the leaves with sure movements, like a man who'd done it a thousand times.

"Toxic. Ain't fit for cookin' or eatin'." He pointed to the small flowers, seemingly harmless under the pale light. "One bite, and you'll be layin' out here before morning."

Paul's smirk faded. *A kid who can't cross a river without panicking, but knows his plants well enough to save a man's life in an instant?*

"Well, damn." Rocco snatched his hand back like he'd nearly grabbed a rattler. "Didn't know I was pickin' my own funeral greens."

Paul stepped closer. "Ain't many hands know that."

Eli kept his head down, his face unreadable. "Learned 'bout plants young. Easier than diggin' graves."

Rocco laughed. "Guess I owe you one, Eli. Might've been a short ride for me otherwise."

"No need for thanks. Just be more careful next time."

Paul narrowed his eyes. "You keepin' any more tricks under your hat?"

"Folks make dumb choices all the time. Learned early, or I'd be buried somewhere by now." Eli bent down again, plucking a different plant from the ground. "If it's greens you're after, this one's safe."

Rocco took the plant with a grin, his eyes darting between Eli and Paul. "Thanks, Eli. Didn't think I'd be gettin' a lesson in plant lore tonight."

Paul patted his angora chaps. "Strange how a man near drowns one day, then's savin' folks the next."

Eli's jaw twitched, betraying his calm exterior. He forced a tight-lipped smile. "Maybe I'm just full of surprises."

Paul didn't flinch, but he knew what he saw—the cracks. Eli was holding up well, but too many things didn't add up. A man who had been under fire, who'd seen the kind of blood Paul had, would wear his lies better. Paul had learned long ago to trust what wasn't being said.

Grunting, Paul turned toward the fire. The air held a bite, and the fire's warmth hardly reached past their circle.

Paul sat back, keeping his distance from the rest of the crew, letting them talk while he kept to his thoughts. Old habits.

Rocco stirred the pot, his grin never far from the surface. He ladled out soup, his eyes lighting on Eli.

"So, Eli..." Rocco leaned in, grinning wide. "Where'd you serve? Can't imagine a man like you sittin' out the war. Bet you got some stories, huh?"

Paul's hand clenched around his cup. The war. That damned war. Rocco always brought it up like it was a fireside tale, something to pass the time. But Paul knew differently. The dead didn't care for stories. He looked at Eli, whose fingers stilled around his tin cup.

"Fought, yeah." Eli's voice, normally sharp as a fresh-sharpened knife, held a dulled edge now.

"Yeah? Where at?"

Eli's eyes darted to the flames. "Rode with a Texas unit," he answered quickly. *Too quickly.* "Stayed south."

South. Paul's brows tightened beneath the brim of his hat. South meant endless marches, skirmishes that turned dirt to mud and men to bones. Paul knew those fields well.

Eli's tone didn't match a man who'd been in them.

Paul narrowed his eyes. "What outfit you run with?"

Eli's hand twitched. He dropped the tin cup to his lap. "Fifth Texas Cavalry." The words stumbled out before the cup clanged down, his fingers drumming against the metal with a nervous rhythm.

Paul didn't blink, just let the silence speak for him, let the fire pop and send embers into the night sky.

"Funny," he said after a beat. "I rode with the Texas boys myself for a bit. Ain't never crossed paths with the Fifth."

Eli's jaw tightened, his eyes darting from the fire to Rocco, then back to the ground. "We moved around. Lotta small skirmishes—hard to keep track of 'em all."

Rocco nodded, slurping his soup. "Makes sense. Bet you saw some rough spots."

Paul didn't take his eyes off Eli. "Sure was. War cuts deep." He paused, then added casually, "Ever cross Harrison's crew? They were holed up near San Antone a spell."

Eli blinked, his spoon frozen halfway to his mouth. "Yeah, sure. Good crew, from what I recall."

Paul leaned back. He didn't need to hear more. Harrison's crew had never made it near San Antonio. They'd never left east Texas, nowhere close to where Eli claimed he'd been.

Rocco chuckled, shaking his head. "Man, I bet you and Paul here could trade stories for hours. War sure leaves a mark, don't it?"

Eli gave a tight nod, his grip tightening around the spoon. "Leaves a scar."

Paul heard more in that tone than Eli probably meant to show. He let the moment stretch, his mind already working. The lie was laid bare, but Paul wasn't going to call Eli on it.

Not yet.

Instead, he looked at Marcus. "Marcus, that freeze by the Red River... reckon you ain't forgot."

Marcus, quiet until now, looked up from his meal. "Reckon I do. Lost half the herd to that damn cold." He spat on the ground, wiping his mouth with the back of his hand. "Wasn't nothin' we could do but ride it out."

Paul nodded.

The winter of '73 had been bitter. Paul's own trail had lost more than half the herd that year. He could still recall the endless days of snow and ice, the cattle falling one by one, their bodies strewn across the frozen plains—markers of their futile journey. The cold had numbed not just his fingers, but his resolve, making each step feel like a battle against nature itself.

Paul had found his resolve and seen it through back then. It had strengthened him. It had strengthened everyone that had gone through it. Yet, Marcus—who had not only gone through it, but wasn't the type to miss details in general—hadn't said a word when Eli spun his lies.

Why? Why keep his secrets?

The wind shifted, carrying with it the faint howl of the wild. It reminded Paul of the time his father had spent teaching him how to track in the wilderness, back when the Texas hills were still his playground, not the battleground they became. Before *her.*

Get out of my mind, damn you.

Later, as the night settled into the kind of quiet that made a man feel the weight of the wilderness pressing down on him, Paul lay apart from the rest of the camp, as was his habit. His bedroll seemed more constrictive than usual, though, and the low crackle of the dying fire reached him like the last whispers of a day's hard ride. Eyes shut, his body ached for sleep, but his mind wouldn't quit.

He exhaled slowly, shoving the memories back down. They always clawed up at night—flashes of Texas fields soaked in blood, old comrades' voices lost to time, *her* face—the woman who'd slipped away with the war's end, leaving nothing but a bitter taste in his mouth. That wound still sat heavy, like the cold metal of a rifle slung across his back. Loss, it seemed, was something he'd never outrun.

Just as sleep started to claim him, the air shifted, almost imperceptibly at first, but Paul's instincts picked it out. A rustle. *Too deliberate for wind.*

He didn't open his eyes, didn't need to. His hand moved on reflex, fingers curling around the grip of his Colt as his heartbeat quickened, each thud clear in the quiet.

His eyes snapped open just as the shadow fell over him.

Eli?

A shovel swung through the air, and the metallic crack of the blade striking solid ground sliced through the stillness. Paul shot upright, gun half-drawn, heart pounding against his ribs.

Eli stood over him, shovel raised. The fire, distant and dim, threw long shadows across his face.

Paul's gaze shifted from Eli to the ground near his bedroll. There, coiled like death itself, lay a rattlesnake, its head severed clean from its body.

Eli wiped the sweat from his brow, stepping back from the dead snake casually.

Paul holstered his gun, the weight of it familiar, reassuring. His voice came low, steady. "Didn't catch it."

"Would've bit you," Eli said simply, crouching as he nudged the snake's severed head with the blade.

Paul's jaw tightened. He wasn't the type to be caught off guard, not by something as simple as a snake. But here he was, owing Eli for saving him from the unseen threat.

He rubbed the back of his neck, the skin prickling from more than just the cold night air. "You always carry that shovel?"

Eli glanced at the shovel, then at Paul, as if weighing whether to answer truthfully or offer another easy lie. "Never know what you'll need on the trail," he said finally. "This time, it came in handy."

A bitter laugh escaped Paul as he stood, stretching out the stiffness in his legs. "Handy enough, I reckon." He let his eyes linger on Eli, watching the firelight flicker over his soft features. A boy like Eli, full of contradictions, must have quite

29

a story beneath the surface. "You always show up just in time, stoppin' things folks don't see?"

Eli's lips twitched into a smile, but it was hollow, like something worn for show. "Luck, I reckon." He tossed the shovel aside, letting it clatter against the dirt.

Paul watched him closely. "Funny how you go from drownin' one day to killin' rattlers like you've been doin' it all your life."

"People surprise you sometimes."

Paul's eyes narrowed. "Ain't that the truth."

"Don't lose sleep over it. Just mind where you lay next time." Eli's voice had a finality to it, like he'd already decided the conversation was over. He moved toward the edge of camp, where the darkness swallowed him whole.

Chapter Three

Fort Reno

Paul's eyes drifted over Fort Reno's weathered walls, and he felt a familiar tightening in his chest. Places like this always reminded him of what he'd lost—his father's sudden death, the war that took everything, and that hollow homecoming to a ranch half-burned and a fiancée already gone East. He'd rebuilt that ranch from the ashes, but the emptiness lingered.

He stole a glance at Rocco and Jody, their easy banter rising above the clatter of hooves.

All he had was silence.

Of course, silence suited him fine, but something about Eli's twitchy movements didn't sit right.

Paul nudged his white mare, Dusty Rose, closer—not quite shielding the boy, but near enough to offer unspoken protection. Whatever had Eli rattled, it had teeth, and Paul had no patience for spooked men.

"Hold steady," Paul said. "Ain't no noose waitin' for ya."

Eli's eyes darted toward the soldiers lounging by the gate. The uniforms, the easy laughs—things a man ought to shrug off—but Eli shrank back.

One of them called out with a friendly laugh, "Hey, gents! Grab a drink with us later?"

Eli flinched, his body recoiling as if the words themselves were a threat.

"You always twitchy 'round uniforms?" Paul asked. "Been to plenty o' forts, I reckon."

"Ain't *my* kind of folks."

Eli's eyes followed the soldiers warily, like a man hunted for desertion. However, Paul knew Eli hadn't been in the war.

"There somethin' you ain't tellin'?"

The boy glanced at him before spurring his horse forward.

Paul rode with quiet confidence, his frame taller than most of the men in the fort. A few soldiers gave him nods of respect. The cut of his weathered buckskin jacket stretched over his broad shoulders, and he imagined that his beard only added to the rugged image of a man used to the wilderness.

As they approached the trading post, they found Aldo waiting, his arms crossed over his chest. He was a squat man, with a face like old leather left out too long in the sun—creased, weather-beaten, skin cracked from years of hard living under the wide sky.

Paul and Eli dismounted and approached him.

"About time you showed," Aldo grumbled. "Was only expectin' one of you. Didn't figure on both."

Paul knew what was coming; Aldo had never been one for fair deals. The kid sure as hell wasn't going to like what Aldo had to say next.

"Only need one of ya, though," Aldo said. "Whoever takes the cattle the rest of the way gets the pay."

Eli's straightened, fists clenching at his sides. "That's a load of bull!"

Paul didn't have to look to know the anger simmering in Eli's face. The boy was too desperate. He'd lost his cool, and Aldo could smell it. Men like that could sniff weakness out a mile away and play it to their advantage.

"Didn't think I was payin' for two. Whoever made it here first would've gotten it all." Aldo's laugh was rough, a rasp that barely escaped his throat. "No need for grifters."

"Ain't how the deal was struck," Eli snapped back.

Paul shot a glance at Eli; he wouldn't win this fight. The boy had guts, but courage didn't mean much in a crooked deal like this. Pushing too hard against men like Aldo only ended one way—broke and bitter. Paul could've mentioned the kid's poor decision on the Washita crossing that had almost lost them cattle and got him drowned. *That'd get me the pay.*

But that wasn't how he worked. You didn't throw a man under the wagon like that.

"Aldo," Paul murmured. "We'll chew on that."

"Suit yourself. Ain't gonna wait long, though."

Paul tugged Eli's arm and pulled him toward the saloon. "C'mon. Let's get a drink and sort this out."

Paul didn't say much as they walked, but he'd seen something different in Eli today—something desperate. He wasn't sure what it was yet, but he planned to find out.

The saloon buzzed with low chatter and clinking glasses, and the smell of old wood and whiskey clung to the air. Paul sat back in his chair, boots planted firmly on the ground. Across from him, Eli fiddled with his tin cup, tracing patterns on the table as if lost in thought.

That twitch had returned—the one that always came when the subject got too close to something Eli didn't want to talk about.

Paul leaned forward, elbows resting on his knees. He wasn't about to let Eli stay quiet forever. The kid had been running since the day they'd met, but the past always had a way of catching up.

"Ain't told me what you're runnin' from yet. No family. No past."

Eli's grip tightened on the cup, the leather of his gloves creaking softly. "Nothin' worth speakin' on."

"That right?" Paul picked up his glass, swirling the amber liquid. This wasn't a new conversation. Every man out here had ghosts. Eli's were just buried deeper than most. "Funny thing—out here, no one's keen to tell their story."

Eli's hand twitched toward the collar of his shirt, fingers brushing against a scar that crept from beneath the fabric, jagged and pale pink—like a burn—against his skin. He didn't seem to realize he was doing it. His eyes darted to the door, as if he'd mapped out every inch of the room, every route to escape. *Like a hunted man.*

"I got my reasons."

"Those reasons got names, or you just runnin' from shadows?"

"Ghosts, maybe." For a moment, it looked like Eli might get up, but he only slumped back and stared into his cup. "Ain't a thing to do about 'em."

Paul leaned back in his chair, his square jaw clenched. "Ghosts don't make no man work a trail or face down a rattler. That's a man runnin' from somethin' real." He paused, watching as Eli's eyes caught the flickering shadows cast by the fire. "We're all runnin'."

Eli's head jerked up. "What'd you run from?"

"War." The word fell heavy between them. "Left plenty behind. Some things don't stay buried."

"Saw my share o' blood."

"Is that right? Where?"

Eli's gaze darted to the door of the saloon. "I told you. Texas Cavalry."

"Funny... Ain't a lot of 'em where you claim." Paul let the silence drag, watching Eli shift uncomfortably in his seat. "Stop diggin' that hole."

Eli's fingers tightened until his knuckles went white.

"Ain't here to drag nothin' from you. But secrets get folks killed. A man's got to know who he's ridin' with." Paul gave the boy a chance to speak, but he stayed quiet, so Paul leaned forward and lowered his voice. "Ain't gonna ask again."

"I ain't a soldier," Eli said, "but I've seen enough to know what that means."

Paul nodded. They sat in silence for a while, the noise of the saloon filling the gap in conversation. Paul let his gaze drift to the scars on Eli's neck again.

"Who did that to you?"

Eli's hand shot up, tugging his collar up. His face darkened, and for a moment, Paul thought he wouldn't answer. Then, the kid cleared his throat and looked away. "Someone who ain't done lookin' for me."

Paul nodded; the pieces were starting to fall into place. He didn't push Eli further, recognizing the signs of a man who'd been through hell and back. Another silence stretched between them, and Paul decided they both had ghosts that weren't ready to be laid to rest.

Eli's voice broke the quiet after a long moment. "You got anyone waitin' for you?"

"No," Paul said flatly, hoping to stave off any talk about his own past. He stared into his glass, the weight of unspoken stories hanging between them.

Eli didn't press.

They sat like that for a while longer, the saloon's noise fading into the background as they shared a silence that spoke louder than words ever could.

The distant sounds of laughter faded as Paul and Eli left the fort behind. As they approached their camp, raised voices sliced through the stillness—angry, aggressive.

"That ain't right," Paul muttered, his hand drifting toward the knife at his belt. His stride lengthened, boots thudding against the hard-packed earth.

Eli's eyes narrowed, and without a word, he broke into a sprint, gravel crunching under his feet.

They rounded a cluster of bushes to find a group of soldiers shoving Marcus, Rocco, and Jody around the campfire.

A soldier with a bushy beard grabbed Jody by the collar. "Think you can cheat us?"

Before Paul could react, Eli launched himself into the fray. "Let him go!"

Eli's shoulder hit Bushy Beard's chest, sending them both crashing to the ground. A soldier with a lazy eye swung at Paul, but he ducked low, and the fist sailed over his head. He came up with a swift uppercut, his knuckles connecting with Lazy Eye's jaw.

The kid moved faster than Paul would've guessed, ducking and weaving with a ferocity that didn't match his delicate frame.

For a moment—just a moment—Paul felt something twist in his chest. Admiration, maybe. Frustration, definitely. The kid obviously didn't have the sense to stay out of trouble, but a fire burned in him, something raw and unrefined.

Paul charged forward, grabbing a soldier with a torn hat who was reaching for his pistol.

"You ain't pullin' that!"

He wrenched the weapon away and tossed it into the shadows. He shoved Torn Hat backward, over a log, then whirled as a shout rang out.

"Get off me!" Rocco was wrestling a soldier with a black mustache, who was trying to pin him down. He drove his elbow into the man's ribs and twisted free, scrambling to his feet.

Rocco's broad chest heaved as he regained his footing, his heavy frame moving with surprising agility. His fists, hardened from years of hard labor, clenched as he eyed the soldier.

Marcus swung a thick branch like a club, keeping two soldiers at bay. "Stay back!"

Suddenly, a soldier sporting a red bandana lunged at Paul with a knife. Paul sidestepped smoothly, grabbing the man's wrist and twisting it sharply.

"Bad idea," he said, forcing Red Bandana to drop the blade before shoving him aside.

Eli rolled across the ground, grappling a soldier with yellow teeth. Yellow Teeth landed a punch to his side, but Eli retaliated with a swift knee to the stomach, pushing the man off.

Jody grabbed a pot of boiling water from the fire. "Back away!" His hands trembled slightly as he held the pot, his wiry frame tense. His freckles stood out even more against his flushed face, the exertion of the scuffle showing in the quick rise and fall of his narrow chest.

Marcus brandished his branch as the soldiers hesitated, eyeing the steaming pot in Jody's hands.

"Enough!"

The soldiers froze as a lieutenant strode into the flickering light, his crisp uniform seeming out of place amid the chaos.

Paul released the soldier he'd been holding, eyes fixed on the officer. "Your boys kicked it off."

The lieutenant glared at his troops. "Back to your posts. Now!"

Muttering, the soldiers backed away, shooting hostile glances at Paul and his crew. One spat on the ground before turning.

Eli pushed himself off the ground, breathing hard, fists still clenched. His shirt was torn, a scrape visible on his forearm.

"Apologies for my men's behavior." The lieutenant tipped his hat. "Won't happen again."

Paul gave a terse nod.

With a final, stern look at his soldiers, the lieutenant marched away. The soldiers trudged after him, some shooting dark looks over their shoulders, and the group disappeared into the darkness.

The camp fell silent except for the crackling of the fire and rustle of movement as they set about putting the camp to rights.

Rocco picked up his hat and smacked it against his thigh, sending a puff of dust into the air. "Well, that was a fine mess." His sun-scorched skin glistened with sweat, inviting the dust to settle in the lines etched into his weathered face.

Jody set the pot back on the fire with shaking hands. "They came out of nowhere." He vibrated with nervous energy, his thin fingers twitching as he fidgeted with the pot's handle.

Marcus exhaled loudly, leaning his makeshift club against a tree. "Everyone alright?"

Paul glanced around until his eyes settled on Eli. "You moved fast."

Eli met his gaze briefly. "Ain't lettin' anyone hurt our crew."

Paul nodded to the scrape on Eli's arm. "You're cut."

"Just a scratch."

Rocco chuckled. "Didn't know you had that fight in you, Eli."

"Sometimes, you don't get a choice." Eli took a scrap of linen from the wagon and tied it around his arm.

Paul helped Jody right a tipped-over crate. "What were they after?"

Jody sighed. "Started asking about our gear, then got pushy when we wouldn't share our provisions."

Marcus shook his head and kicked dirt over the trampled area near the fire. "Soldiers thinking they can take what they like."

"Not while we're around," Paul declared.

Eli glanced toward the fort. "We should stay sharp tonight."

Paul nodded. "I'll take first watch."

Chapter Four

Fort Reno

Elsie bolted upright in her bedroll, her heart pounding against her ribs. Her eyes swept across the camp—Paul's spot was empty.

He's gone to Aldo—making the deal, probably telling him about how I almost drowned.

As she reached for her boots, a pit opened in her stomach, twisting into something sharp and cold. Of *course* he was cutting her out—why wouldn't he? She should've known better than to trust him, or anyone, for that matter. Men like Paul were practical, survivalists, and they didn't take dead weight along for the ride.

That's all I am—baggage.

Jonathan had said as much, hadn't he? *"You're only good for one thing."*

She couldn't let that be her reality anymore. She had to stop Paul before he sealed her fate. She had to fight for this one chance to be free of Jonathan.

"Need help?"

Elsie flinched, her hands freezing mid-motion, and turned to see Marcus approaching. There was no mockery in his tone, no probing questions. Just an offer.

"I'm fine." She focused on her feet, tugging her boots on.

Marcus didn't push, just lingered a moment longer before nodding. "All right," he murmured. "If you need a hand, I'm here."

She nodded, threw her hat on, and rushed off.

Her boots scuffed against the dirt as she stumbled through camp, tripping over the uneven ground as she rushed toward Fort Reno. The shadows of early morning stretched long over the wooden buildings, but she ignored them, pushing forward, her breath quickening.

Her steps faltered when she reached the trading post. Boards creaked beneath her boots as she crept up the stairs. Pressing her ear against the door, she could hear muffled voices inside.

"Fair's fair," Paul said, his voice low but clear through the thin wood. "We both worked it. Splittin' the pay makes sense."

Elsie's fists clenched, her knuckles white. She pressed harder against the door, straining to catch every word.

"I ain't one for charity," Aldo grumbled. "You sure that kid can hold up his end? Seems a bit... green."

"Maybe, but Eli's proven himself. He'll hold."

He's backing me up? Not cutting her out, but offering to split the fee. Why? He knew she wasn't fit for the trail. *So why help?*

"Fine," Aldo grunted. "Half the pay, but if anything goes wrong—"

"I'll take responsibility."

Elsie couldn't make sense of it—Paul was sticking his neck out for her. He wasn't leaving her behind, wasn't cutting her out. Not only was he was offering to split the payment, but he'd offered to take the blame if things went south.

But why? What could he possibly gain?

It didn't sit right with her. Men didn't do things out of the goodness of their hearts—not the men she'd known, anyway. After all, Jonathan had been kind at first, saying all the right things, even after he'd taken her from her father's ranch by force. Then, just when she'd let her guard down, the mask had slipped.

The conversation inside the trading post wound down, and Elsie realized she needed to move unless she wanted to get caught eavesdropping.

She retreated into the shadows.

What did Paul want from her? The more she thought about it, the less she liked it. *I can't trust him—can't trust anyone.*

Yet, as much as her mind told her to walk away, to protect herself, a small part of her wanted to believe he was different.

She hated that part, had kept it buried deep. It made her weak.

Paul strode out of the trading post, his hat pulled low as the sun bathed the street in harsh light.

Elsie stepped in front of him. "What'd you get outta that?"

Paul's lips twitched. "You always listen behind doors, or is today special?"

Elsie's cheeks burned, but she refused to back down. Crossing her arms over her chest, she narrowed her eyes. "You could've just kept it. Ain't like I'm pullin' my weight."

Paul studied her for a long moment, his expression unreadable, though something softened in his eyes. "We balance out. I hunt. You're better at camp, foragin'. I can teach you the rest."

Elsie blinked, caught off guard. She opened her mouth to argue, but the words died in her throat.

She wasn't sure whether to feel insulted or relieved. She could hunt—not well, maybe, but she could lay snares, and she'd caught plenty rabbits in her time. And foraging? Her father had taught her long ago what plants were edible and which would kill you, though she wasn't about to share that little detail.

Still, her meager skills weren't enough out here. Not enough to stop her heart from pounding every time she heard a twig snap in the dark or a mysterious rustle too close for comfort.

"Workin' together gets it done quicker, which means we get paid sooner." Paul's hands rested easily at his sides; apparently, this conversation wasn't rattling him the way it was her.

"Don't see why. You don't owe me nothin'."

"I don't do things out of pity, Eli. If you weren't worth it, I wouldn't bother."

"But—" she began, then hesitated, biting her lip. "You don't even know me."

"Maybe not, but you've held up. I seen enough to know you ain't just some greenhorn."

She almost told him about the sprig of yarrow she'd tucked into her pocket that morning, how she'd noticed the patch of dandelion greens behind the camp, perfect for boiling up in a stew. She'd learned a lot from her father, back before everything went to hell—how to recognize the sweet scent of wild mint, how to avoid the false promises of nightshade berries.

But quick as the impulse to speak came, the memory of Jonathan's cigar and his screams of *"Don't brag about what didn't come from me!"* echoed through her mind.

"Don't need no handholdin'." That was all she could bring herself to say. "I can figure it."

"Maybe, but no need to make it harder. Ain't no shame in learnin'."

Elsie's lips pressed into a thin line. Her pride stung, but he wasn't mocking her, or even pushing her. He was just... offering.

She exhaled slowly, her body relaxing despite herself. "Fine," she muttered. "For now."

Paul nodded.

The two of them made their way out of Fort Reno. As they walked, Elsie overheard a group of soldiers talking among themselves.

"Gangs movin' north out of Texas."

The words hit her like a hammer, and suddenly, the open air felt suffocating, as though the walls of the fort were creeping in closer. The clink of spurs echoed too loudly, too shrilly in her ears, like the ghosts of Jonathan's men were right there, just out of sight.

It had to be Jonathan's gang. She had no idea how he'd tracked her so far north, but it couldn't be anyone else. He'd always been relentless in his pursuit of her, and each time he'd caught her brought fresh burns and fresh scars.

The ground seemed to tilt beneath her, the horizon swaying in and out of focus. She couldn't breathe. The sunlight felt oppressive, burning into her skin, her chest tightening with every breath. She tried to block it out, to focus on something—anything—but the more she fought, the more the panic rose, like a wave threatening to pull her under.

She didn't dare imagine what would happen if Jonathan caught her this time.

"Hey." Paul gripped her arm with his large hand. "Eyes on me."

Elsie's breath came in ragged gasps, her eyes darting around wildly before she forced herself to meet his gaze.

Jonathan's voice echoed in her ears, low and rough, each word a lash against her skin. She remembered the way he'd cornered her in the barn, the heat of his breath on her neck as he whispered promises she had no choice but to accept. "*You're mine,*" he'd said, his grip like iron on her arm. "*You ain't goin' nowhere.*" The burn of his hand, the way he'd twisted her wrist until she felt something crack—she could still feel it, even now, like a ghost haunting every step she took.

She'd run then, the fear driving her forward. But no matter how far she got, she could never seem to outrun the memory of that voice.

Paul's hand tightened on her arm, the warmth of his touch pulling her back, grounding her in the moment. The roar of her thoughts still surged in her ears, but slowly, her vision cleared.

"Easy now," he murmured. "Breathe."

Elsie tried, but this was... *wrong.*

His hand—the warm and solid hand that anchored her—was *wrong*.

It wasn't supposed to be like this. Men's hands *hurt*—they took, they bruised, they left scars that never fully faded.

However, something about Paul's grip was different, steady in a way that made her chest ache. It was infuriating how her body leaned toward that warmth, how some long-forgotten part of her wanted to curl up and just... rest.

"What's goin' on?" he asked.

"Nothing." Elsie flexed her trembling fingers. "I'm fine."

"Ain't lookin' fine. Somethin' got to you."

I can't tell him. Not about the gang, not about the danger she was running from.

"I'm just..." She paused. "Just tired. That's all."

"If there's somethin' to say, say it now."

Elsie's small hands fidgeted with the brim of her hat. Her short hair curled damply at the nape of her neck, itching under the collar. Her oversized jacket weighed on her shoulders, feeling heavy and unnatural against her body.

She shook her head. "It's nothin'. Let's keep movin'."

Paul's gaze lingered on her for a moment longer before he gave a slow nod. "Alright."

He resumed his stride, and Elsie followed him. Her legs felt like half-cooked noodles, but she forced herself to keep moving. The noise of the fort faded behind them as they made their way back to camp.

"There's a gang leader after me," she blurted suddenly.

The words had slipped out before she could stop them, and the moment they left her mouth, regret slammed into her, fast and hard.

What have I done?

She wasn't supposed to trust anyone, wasn't supposed to let anyone get close. Jonathan had taught her *that* lesson well. Men took what they wanted and left you broken when they were through.

Her chest tightened again, but not from panic this time—from the weight of her own stupidity. She'd let her guard down, let Paul see too much.

And yet... the warmth of his hand on her arm lingered, steady and sure, grounding her in a way that both infuriated and comforted her.

She hated it. Resented that he could make her feel safe, even for a second.

She yanked her hat lower, biting down against the bile rising in her throat.

Paul stiffened. His steps faltered, but he didn't stop walking. His face was a careful blank. "That what brought you out here?"

Elsie's breath hitched in her throat, and she nodded quickly, swallowing hard. "I don't want to talk about it."

She wasn't ready to go any deeper. *Not yet.*

Paul seemed to take her at her word. "Fair 'nuff." He examined her face for another moment before nodding. "We'll handle it."

The words were simple, almost casual, but they settled over her like a heavy blanket—cozy but suffocating.

Does he mean it? Or is he just saying it to get me to shut up, to stop trembling like a fool?

Images of what could happen came unbidden, sharp and brutal—the leering faces of Jonathan's men, their hands grabbing at her, dragging her back into the darkness she'd fought so hard to escape.

They won't stop at me. They'd go through Paul, through anyone who got in their way. She knew what they were capable of. She'd seen it. Felt it. And the thought of Paul standing between her and them? It scared her almost as much as the gang itself.

She gritted her teeth, steeling herself for what was coming. Because no matter what Paul said, no matter how safe she felt for now, they were coming.

Elsie tugged at the brim of her hat again, hiding the storm of emotion that must have crept into her eyes. "Thanks."

It wasn't much, but it was all she could offer.

Paul didn't respond right away—just kept walking, his gaze fixed ahead—but after a moment, he gave a slight nod. "Ain't no need for thanks."

Chapter Five

Near El Reno

Paul led the group north, his eyes scanning the horizon, but his mind was elsewhere. A man named Bailey had joined them only hours ago, riding in with a grin that Paul hadn't trusted from the moment he saw it.

Aldo had sent word, said they'd need another hand... but Paul couldn't shake the unease gnawing at him.

Bailey rode up beside him, twirling his rifle like it was some kind of toy. "Hell of a day, huh?"

"Ain't over yet."

Abruptly, Bailey lifted his rifle and aimed at a rabbit scurrying across the dirt. With a loud crack, the rabbit fell limp.

"Got 'im!"

Bailey's wiry build and lanky limbs made him seem taller than he was, but the careless way he went about his work grated on Paul's nerves. *Chucklehead seems to think that everything could be done with a lick and a promise.* Paul may look wild, with his dense beard and furs, but at least he stayed clean; Bailey's greasy hair hung in uneven strands that obscured his jaundiced eyes, a dull shade of brown that, in the right light, resembled the mud caking his boots.

Bailey laughed, holstering the rifle with practiced ease. "Clean shot, huh?"

Paul's jaw tightened, the muscles in his neck coiling with frustration. The lunkhead killed for fun, and it grated on him.

Another shot rang out not long after, downing another rabbit. Bailey's laughter echoed again, but this time, Paul reined Dusty Rose in, stopping dead in his tracks.

"Get down. Fetch it," Paul growled.

Bailey's laughter died quickly, his grin fading as he gaped at Paul. A challenge flickered in Bailey's eyes, but Paul's hand hovered near his holster, his stance unwavering.

Bailey shifted in his saddle, the smile returning but colder now, sharp. "You serious?"

"Serious as a curly wolf."

Bailey hesitated, glaring, but Paul didn't budge. Finally, with a reluctant grunt, Bailey swung down from his horse, landing with a thud. He shuffled over to the rabbit, kicking up dust, and bent down to pick it up.

"Waste of time." Bailey tossed the rabbit into his saddlebag as the others watched on wordlessly.

"You kill it, you fetch it."

Bailey mounted his horse again, wiping sweat from his brow. "You're the boss."

His voice dripped with sarcasm, but anger simmered beneath the surface, lending an edge to his tone that Paul didn't miss.

As they rode on, Paul's hand stayed close to his holster. He wanted Bailey to know exactly where they stood. He glanced back once, catching Eli watching from a distance. The kid was keeping his distance from Bailey, but Paul couldn't blame him. Something about Bailey was off, and it wasn't just the killing for sport.

Bailey's skin bore a sallow undertone, and his eyes had a yellowish tint to them; bloodshot veins crept toward the irises, giving him a perpetually mean, half-crazed look.

Turning those jaundiced eyes toward Paul, Bailey smirked. "You always so serious, Boone? Seems to me a man could use a little fun on the trail."

"Ain't no fun in what needs doin'. Job comes first."

"Job's gettin' done just fine."

"I'm runnin' this outfit. It goes my way."

Bailey let out a short, bitter laugh, but he didn't argue. His taunting grin lingered, but the man's smile never quite seemed to reach his eyes.

Paul had seen that look before—men who played with rattlesnakes just to feel the bite.

Bailey shifted in the saddle, his fingers tapping a restless rhythm on the stock of his rifle. The man's gaze swept the horizon—not like a trail hand, but like a predator sizing up the land, seeking out the weak spots.

Paul had ridden with a man like that once, back in '64—a wobble-jaw who'd laugh even as bullets whistled past. That joker had laughed all the way up until the day he got two of Paul's men shot.

I ain't lettin' history repeat itself.

The herd ambled along steadily, kicking up dust as the sky began to darken. Keeping one eye on the cattle, Paul scanned the landscape to read the subtle dips and rises in the terrain. The land spoke in ways most men didn't bother to listen to, but he'd always felt a connection to the land; over the years, he'd learned to read it like a map—the way the grass bent under a south wind, how the soil turned slick before a downpour.

Paul still remembered the day he'd ignored his instincts, driving a herd through a low valley just before the rain hit. They'd lost twenty head to the floodwaters that followed, the cattle's panicked bawling swallowed by the roar of the rising river.

It was a mistake he wouldn't make twice.

Guiding Dusty away from Bailey, Paul rode up to Eli. "See that dip?" He leaned slightly in his saddle and pointed toward a low stretch of land in the distance. "That'll flood fast. Higher ground's your safe bet when storms roll in."

Eli's eyes followed Paul's finger, his brow furrowing as he squinted at the horizon, where clouds had started to gather. The wind whipped his hat, and Paul could see the flicker of doubt in Eli's movements—hesitant, unsure.

"We'll camp up there." Paul straightened, his hand resting easy on the reins as he nodded toward a ridge up ahead. "Keep the cattle dry. Don't worry. You'll learn the land."

Eli nodded, his fingers tightening on the reins. "Ain't slackin'."

"Didn't say you were." Paul tugged Dusty's reins, guiding her closer to Eli. "You wanna listen anyway. Land don't care 'bout slackin' or tryin'—just smart or dead."

"Thanks." Eli tugged his hat lower as the wind whipped harder. "Ain't lookin' to mess up."

"Messin' up's part of it. Trick's learnin' from it."

Once they'd reached the ridge, Paul swung down from his saddle, his boots sinking into the damp earth as he surveyed the area. The wind had picked up, and the first fat drops of rain were already splattering against the ground.

Eli stood beside his horse, eyes flitting between the cattle and the ridge, like he wasn't sure where to start.

"First thing," Paul said, loosening the ties on his saddle, "we get the herd secured so they don't wander when the storm hits. Fence them in tight against the ridge. Use a natural barrier whenever you can. Saves time, and the land is sturdier than anything a man puts up."

Eli nodded, his hands working to free the rope from his saddle.

Paul tethered Dusty and motioned for Eli to follow. Together, they corralled the cattle up against the natural rock wall. Eli fumbled with the knots at first, but Paul stepped in, showing him how to loop the rope properly.

"Keep it snug." Paul tightened the rope around a post. "You don't want 'em breakin' loose. Seen storms spook a herd worse than wolves."

Eli glanced at the darkening sky, then back at the cattle. "What about a fire?"

Paul shook his head, moving to stake down the last post. "In this wind, we'll need to dig a trench—keep it low to the ground, use the rocks around us as cover. Fire won't do us any good if the first gust blows it out."

He led Eli to a spot sheltered by a cluster of boulders, knelt to pick up a sharp stone, and dug into the soft earth. The wind howled above them, but here, in the shadow of the ridge, they were protected.

Eli watched for a moment, then crouched, mimicking Paul. His hands moved clumsily, but with each stroke, the trench took shape.

"You ain't done this before, have you?" Paul asked, glancing sideways at Eli.

Eli's face was set in concentration. "Not like this."

Paul grunted. "You'll learn. Out here, the land teaches you quick—don't matter how smart you are, you listen or you end up dead."

They finished the trench just as rain started coming down in earnest, hitting the ground in heavy bursts. Paul grabbed the tarp from his saddle, handing Eli one end while he held the other.

"Now, this part's important," Paul said, his voice calm even as the wind whipped, tugging at the canvas. "Tie it off low, stretch it tight, and angle it down. If your tarp sags, water'll pool inside and drown the fire. Seen men freeze to death 'cause they didn't bother to secure their shelter."

Eli pulled the rope taut, securing it as Paul demonstrated. The wind yanked at the edges of the tarp, but with both of them working together, it soon held firm, forming a sloped cover shielding the trench.

Paul stood back, eyes scanning their setup. "Not bad," he said, wiping the rain from his brow. "It'll hold."

Eli looked up, rain dripping from the brim of his hat. "Thanks."

Paul nodded once, satisfied, though he knew Eli still had a long way to go. That was fine. Paul wasn't in any hurry. He'd teach Eli what he needed to know, one lesson at a time.

The storm rolled in with a vengeance, lightning cracking across the sky, the resulting thunder shaking the ground like cannon fire. The tent flap rattled, the rapid-fire tapping like the staccato burst of gunfire.

Paul's hand drifted to his holster, fingers wrapping around the worn leather grip of his revolver.

He'd done this a thousand times—lying in the mud, rain slicking his hair, waiting for the next shot, the next order. He hadn't been able to sleep without his gun close since Gettysburg. Of course, this wasn't the same, but his body didn't know that. It only knew the way his heart kicked up, the way every nerve went taut, ready to spring.

Old habits. Old damn habits.

Paul lay on his back, trying to ignore the sound, willing sleep to come.

His eyes fluttered shut, but flashes of lightning lit the dark tent, each one tugging him closer to darker days. The flash of gunfire in his mind was brighter. The rumble of the storm twisted into the shouts of men, the crack of rifles, and the wet thud of bodies hitting the ground. Paul thrashed in his bedroll, his hands curling into fists, his breathing harsh.

Suddenly, hands gripped his shoulders firmly. Paul jolted awake, instinctively grappling with the weight holding him down. His body moved before his mind caught up, twisting to get free. He was back in the war—fighting, surviving.

"Paul!"

The voice cut through the fog of his nightmare, and his eyes snapped open. Eli was leaning over him, pressing him down, trying to stop him from thrashing.

Paul froze, trembling. *When did he come in?*

They stared at each other, both breathing hard, tension thick in the air.

Paul's heart hammered as he blinked, reality crashing back in. He let out a slow breath, his muscles finally relaxing as he realized where he was. Releasing his grip on Eli's arms, he sat up, dragging a shaky hand through his damp hair.

Eli shifted back, giving him space, but didn't say a word. His face was pale in the flickering lantern light, his chest heaving. Outside, thunder cracked, but inside the tent, it was quiet.

"War dreams." The words came out before Paul could stop them, rougher than he intended. "Tommy Graves. Barely nineteen. Swore up and down that locket of his kept him safe."

Paul could still see it—Tommy had clutched that locket even as the life bled out of him, eyes wide, uncomprehending, as if it had lied to him in the end. There were others, too—faces that blurred together, names that never quite left him. It wasn't the deaths that haunted him; it was the way they'd looked to him for answers he didn't have, the way they expected him to make it right.

"Didn't matter what I did." He couldn't bring himself to meet Eli's eye. He didn't need sympathy. He just needed the words out. "Lost 'em anyway."

Eli sat quietly, letting him talk.

Rubbing a hand over his beard, Paul sighed. "Ain't ever easier."

Silence stretched between them, softer now. Eli didn't push, and Paul didn't offer, but something had shifted—an understanding, wordless but there.

Paul's pulse slowed as the memories faded.

"Appreciate it," he mumbled.

Eli gave a small nod.

Eli wrapped his arms around his knees, eyes distant. He hadn't said much since waking Paul—neither of them were the type to push for words when silence would do.

"Saved me from that snake." Paul chuckled faintly. "Now this."

Eli's lips twitched into a smile, and he looked down.

"The men I lost..." Paul sighed. "They were under *my* command. Good men."

Eli shifted, his fingers brushing absently over the scars on his neck, the old burns Paul had noticed before. The kid didn't say anything about it, but the movement was enough to catch Paul's eye.

They were both carrying things—different scars, but the weight was the same.

"If you ever want to talk about it, I'll listen," Paul murmured.

Eli's eyes rose to meet his. He didn't say anything, but his slight nod was enough.

Paul leaned back, pulling his coat tighter. The fire was stronger now, its warmth spreading through the tent. The storm had quieted, leaving behind the soft sounds of the night. For the first time in a long while, Paul felt a flicker of peace.

He and Eli weren't just trail partners anymore. Something deeper had taken root, something Paul couldn't quite name yet—but it was there, and it was growing.

Chapter Six

Jon stood on a small ridge, smoking with Layton and Kid Olson as the rest of his men rushed to finish up with the ranch below—lighting fires, dragging out what little valuables they could find: silver candlesticks, a few pieces of jewelry, a dusty pocket watch, and some family heirlooms. The kind of things people thought they could hide.

There probably would've been more loot if he'd let Kid go down there, but Jon wasn't eager to let Kid around the rest of the men alone.

Jon's Peacemaker hung heavily at his hip, and his gun belt brimmed with loops of.45 caliber rounds.

The clapboard ranch house smoldered, the dry timber snapping and cracking as the flames took hold. The livestock pens rattled with the agitated lowing of cattle, and a jackrabbit darted out from under the porch. A fitting end to whatever pathetic dreams had been built here. People who couldn't defend their property deserved to lose it.

Jon squinted; smoke stung his eyes, but it was satisfying in its own way. This was power—watching what others had built turn into ash because *he* willed it. The trinkets they dragged out were meaningless, but the fear they represented?

That was something he could use.

Hooves approached him from behind, and Jon turned to look.

Jimmy and Edd had finally returned. They'd been gone for weeks, sent to Caldwell to track down that ungrateful hellcat, Elsie. He'd hoped they would bring her back, but he didn't see her. She'd been gone longer than ever before. *Too long.*

Perhaps long enough for people to start thinking Jonathan Rickett couldn't keep his woman under control.

That was a slippery slope into *his* people thinking he couldn't keep *them* under control.

As the pair approached, Edd, an older bald man, slipped off his saddle and crumpled to the ground, unconscious. Jimmy, a wiry young man with a faded bandana around his neck, dismounted and took a few hesitant steps forward.

"Boss," he croaked. "We couldn't find her. Not at the old place. Not anywhere."

Jon's spurs, etched with a scrollwork pattern, chimed with each deliberate step. He stared at Jimmy as he walked. Jimmy's shoulders were slumped, his head bowed. The noise of men looting and setting fires faded into the background.

Jon struck Jimmy, landing a solid blow to the face. As his fist connected, Jon felt a fleeting flicker of satisfaction. The rage inside him was insatiable, a void that even violence couldn't fill. Jimmy's yelp of pain barely registered.

Why couldn't they just do what they were told? Why couldn't they just be competent? Everything seemed to slip through his fingers lately.

Jimmy stumbled and went down. He opened his mouth, maybe to apologize, but Jon didn't want to hear it. He wanted someone else to suffer under his rage.

Jon pulled the cheroot cigar from his mouth, the end glowing a dull orange in the twilight, and knelt beside Jimmy. The faint scent of tobacco mingled with the acrid smoke from the burning ranch. Jon grinned, and Jimmy gulped.

Jon pressed the glowing tip into Jimmy's cheek as Layton and Kid watched on impassively.

The sizzle, the smell of burning flesh, the scream—it was like white sugar on Jon's tongue. Jimmy writhed beneath him, trying to squirm away, but Jon held him there. Something about how people's eyes widened when they were afraid of him—it made his blood sing. He'd felt it the first time he put a knife to a man's throat and watched his bravado crumble into pleading.

Power was addictive; the more Jon took, the more he craved.

"Four times." Jon drew the cigar back. "Four damn times she's escaped, and now you show up, hands empty, guts useless?"

Jimmy coughed. "She's smart, boss. Real smart. Knows the land better than we thought," he wheezed.

Jon kicked his side. "Shut your mouth!"

His mind boiled with images of Elsie slipping away again and again, outsmarting him at every turn. Heat rose in his chest, a gnawing reminder that it wasn't just her freedom she'd stolen—it was his reputation.

Jon lifted the cigar back to his lips, and the ember flared as he took a long, slow drag.

"We'll find her." Jimmy spat blood on the dust. "We—"

Jon smashed his boot into Jimmy's ribs again.

His father had taught him early—respect was born from fear. Jon remembered the knotted fists that never hesitated to come down on any worker that spoke out of turn, dared to disobey, or was just at the wrong place at the wrong time.

"You'd better." He ground his teeth against the bitterness of doubt. That's what she did to him—left him questioning everyone, everything. "Or maybe I'll start wonderin' if you're helpin' her."

Jimmy's eyes widened. "No! No, boss, I swear—"

Jon leaned down. "You think I can't tell when someone's lyin'? You think I don't know what desperation looks like?"

Jimmy's face went as pale as the desert sand. *Weakness.* That was all Jon saw now, and it sickened him.

Weakness was the thing Jon feared most, a lesson beaten into him by years of hardship. He'd seen what happened to weak men—they were used, taken advantage of, discarded. He'd promised himself he would never be like that. He would take what was his, and he would make sure no one ever had the power to wrest it from him.

Jon straightened. "Get out of my sight."

Once Jimmy had crawled away as quickly as the pain would let him, Layton stepped up next to Jon. His expression was unreadable, his posture relaxed. Layton had always been like that—calm, composed, never giving anything away.

It was as useful as it was irritating.

"You think I shouldn't have done it?" Jon asked.

"I think she's slippery." Layton tilted his head. "Burning our men ain't gonna make findin' her any easier."

"Maybe."

"Just sayin', sometimes a softer hand gets the best results. Not everyone breaks the same way."

Jon looked at him, his jaw tightening. "I don't need no advice on how to handle my men."

"Still think sendin' them to her old man's ranch was pointless. He don't even live there anymore, and the new owner—"

"Pays us for protection. I know!" Jon inhaled sharply. "She had no way of knowin' that. Let it go."

Layton was the closest thing Jon had to a friend, though neither was likely to say. They'd met in the war, both young and full of fire, each with a grudge against the world. Layton had saved Jon's life more than once, but that didn't mean Jon could let him question his authority now. Friendship was one thing, loyalty another.

"Maybe we should head further north. Toward people. Protection."

"She don't need protection." Jon clenched his jaw. "She needs *me*."

Layton raised an eyebrow. "You really think she'd fall in line? After everything?"

"She belongs to me."

He could see it—the way he'd dragged her out of that dusty ranch. Her face had been pale as she'd trembled before him. She'd tried to run, but he'd grabbed her by the hair and yanked her back. He'd broken her and claimed her as his. She was his trophy. He'd treated her well enough.

Better than a woman deserves, in any case.

The first time she'd run off, he hadn't taken it seriously—just a scared girl trying to escape an inescapable fate. He'd brought her back, half-dead and broken. That's when he'd first branded her as his.

I'll do much worse this time.

"You wanna move *north*?" Kid stomped over, his raspy voice laced with the kind of defiance that came from too much whiskey and too many saloon brawls. "Reckon we can high-tail it up there, but what then? Ain't no railroad to bring us back yet."

"What's your point?"

"We keep going north, we'll be gone for months. People'll forget us, Jon. Forget who runs this place."

Jon's hands curled into fists as he got up in Kid's face. Kid stared at him without flinching, his eyes locked on Jon's as if to dare him.

"You got something to say, Kid?" Jon grabbed his collar and yanked him forward. "You think people will forget about *me*?"

Kid held his eyes for a heartbeat, his eyes narrowing, then raised his hands, palms out, a slow grin spreading across his face. His shoulders relaxed, almost like he was daring Jon to make a move.

"What's the matter, Jon? You're all twitchy."

"You think this is a game, Kid? You think this is a joke?"

"I think you're chasin' a ghost, that's all. Seems to me she's long gone, and now you want to leave space for someone to take what's ours?"

"We're gonna find her, come back, and run off any son of a gun that dares enter our territory. You got a problem with that, you can stay right here in this dirt. For good."

No mercy, especially not for deserters. In the war, Jon had been good at following orders, giving orders, making sure no one questioned him. He'd learned that the only way to survive was to be harder than everyone else. The war had stripped

65

him of everything soft, leaving behind a man who only knew how to fight and take.

"No need for that, Jon." Kid's grin faded. "Just making sure we're all on the same page."

Jon shoved him back. "Then shut up and do as you're told."

Kid clicked his tongue and stalked off toward the horses.

Jon had to look strong—had to *be* strong. Anything less, and he was nothing. They all knew that. Weakness spread like blood in the water, and Jon couldn't afford even a hint of it.

Chapter Seven

Near El Reno

The cool air hinted at a long day ahead as Paul tightened the straps on his saddle. His hand found his rifle when he caught sight of Eli approaching, boots kicking up dust with each hesitant step.

Paul cocked his head. "Somethin' on your mind?"

Eli glanced over his shoulder, where Bailey loitered by the fire. "Figured I'd ride along, see if I can't learn somethin'."

Paul narrowed his eyes, knowing exactly why Eli wanted to tag along. Avoiding Bailey was one thing, but Paul didn't like people hiding from their problems. Still, he gave a curt nod, figuring this might give him a chance to get a better read on the kid.

"Saddle up."

They rode out in silence. Paul didn't mind, but he could feel the quiet pressing down on Eli. Every so often, Eli threw a nervous glance over his shoulder, as if expecting Bailey to show up.

This ain't regular fear...

There was something about Eli's unease, the way he moved—like someone bracing for a hit. It stirred memories—not of war, but of people who flinched at shadows, eyes hollowed by things that happened behind closed doors. He could read the signs, could tell when someone had been backed into corners too many times. Eli had that look, but there was more to it.

67

What happened to scare you so bad, kid?

As they neared a herd of buffalo grazing in the distance, Paul slowed Dusty Rose, sliding off her back to crouch low against the ground. He directed Eli to do the same. The buffalo, massive and slow-moving, blended into the earth like boulders.

The wind tugged at Paul's dark, cropped hair, and he adjusted the wide-brimmed hat to shield his face from the harsh sunlight, narrowing his eyes as he surveyed the herd.

"Rule one," he whispered. "Don't fire unless you're sure." He glanced at Eli, who adjusted his rifle. "Rule two: take only what you need."

Eli nodded, his hands on the rifle's stock, but Paul could see the tremble in his grip. Something in the way Eli moved wasn't quite right. Not quite... masculine. The thought gnawed at Paul as the moment stretched out, only deepening Paul's worries about what Eli had suffered in the past.

Or maybe I'm wrong, and his secret is something else entirely...

As Eli raised his rifle, Paul remembered another shot.

It had been a winter's night back in '67, snow piled high around the camp, and a boy about Eli's age had taken a bullet to the leg. Infection had set in quickly, fever hotter than a branding iron... by morning, nothing was left but pain.

Paul had pulled the trigger himself—the first time he'd ever taken a human life outside the heat of battle.

It had stayed with him, clinging to his bones like the cold.

Watching Eli now, Paul felt that same weight settle over him—the burden of what it meant to lead, to teach, to carry the weight of another's choices.

Finally, Eli squeezed the trigger.

The shot rang out, and one of the buffalo staggered before dropping to the ground. The rest of the herd scattered, their hooves thundering against the plains as they fled.

Paul stood and approached the fallen buffalo. Eli followed, and Paul watched him closely, pondering the strange way Eli moved. Eli rattled off all the uses he could think of for buffalo hide, but Paul wasn't listening; he was too busy trying to figure out what Eli was hiding.

Paul knelt to examine the buffalo. "Done this kinda thing before?"

Eli's shoulders stiffened. "Been out a time or two."

He ain't got the confidence of someone who's grown up hunting.

"Is that right?"

The rhythmic scrape of metal against buffalo hide filled the air, blending with the earthy, metallic scent of blood. Paul worked silently, his hands moving with practiced precision as he stripped the hide.

"This gang you're runnin' from..." Paul let the words hang for a moment, his knife pausing mid-cut. "You one of 'em?"

Eli's head snapped up, the knife in his hand forgotten. "No!" The word came out rapidly, like a bullet fired before its time.

Paul didn't flinch. He just waited. The silence grew almost suffocating. Paul kept his gaze locked on the hide, resuming his work with deliberate calm.

Eli's hand tightened around the knife before he looked away. "Took someone from me. I ain't forgivin' 'em for it."

The tremor in Eli's voice was faint, but Paul recognized it immediately. *Grief.* The kind of sorrow that clung to a man long after the dust had settled and never fully left.

Paul's chest tightened, his hands slowing as his own losses flickered through his mind, unbidden. The sounds of men dying with his name on their lips echoed in the back of his head. He swallowed hard, his throat dry.

"Grief don't quit," Paul muttered, more to himself than to Eli. "Sticks with you like a burr."

Eli's movements had slowed, and his earlier sharpness had disappeared, replaced by something more fragile. By the time they'd removed the buffalo's hide and packed the meat away, the sky had begun to darken.

Paul stood, wiping his hands on his trousers, his eyes drifting toward the distant hills. "A friend, then?"

"Yeah." Eli stared at the ground. "Best friend I ever had."

Paul nodded slowly. "Ain't easy, carryin' it. But don't let it rot—it'll eat you hollow."

Eli's jaw tightened, like he might push back; instead, he nodded almost imperceptibly.

Paul mounted Dusty and turned back toward camp.

As they rode, he spotted a wagon, its heavy frame stuck in a deep rut. A family of four scrambled around it, struggling to free the wheels.

Paul could ignore this family—could ride on and leave them to their fate—but that wasn't how he was wired.

He spurred Dusty forward. "Eli, come on. We'll give 'em a hand."

As they approached, the father waved them down, his face lined with stress and exhaustion. "Please, we're stuck. Can't get it out," he panted. "The sun's going down... my family... We don't have much time."

Paul took in the scene quickly. The wagon was buried deep, its wheels sunk almost halfway. He dismounted. "We'll get it done."

Eli jumped down and joined Paul.

Paul crouched beside the wagon, eyeing the wheels buried deep in the rut. He grabbed a length of rope from his saddlebag, handing one end to Eli and looping the other around the back axle.

"Leverage is what gets the job done," Paul said. "Ain't just about pullin'—you gotta make the ground work for you."

He gestured to a nearby boulder. "Run the rope around that rock, like so. Gives you the angle you need. Tension's what lifts it."

Eli fumbled initially, rushing to the point of clumsiness, but Paul placed a hand on his shoulder.

"Easy, there—slow down. You want it snug, but not so tight it'll snap."

Eli nodded, adjusting his grip to loop the rope like Paul showed him.

"Good," Paul said, testing the line. "Now, when I say 'haul,' we pull together. Watch how the wheels shift—don't just yank and hope. The trick ain't in the pull, it's in how you use the weight."

"Got it."

Paul gave the rope a sharp tug, judging the tension, then nodded. "Count it. One... two... Haul!"

Grunting, Paul and Eli pulled, the muscles in their arms straining as the wagon shifted slightly. The wooden wheels groaned against the dirt, but it wasn't enough.

"Again," Paul barked, his hands tightening on the rope. "Haul!"

Eli dug his boots into the ground, twisting his face with effort as they heaved the wagon upward. This time, the wheels jolted free, moving a few inches before settling again.

The father let out a gasp, his eyes wide. "It's movin'! You've almost got it!"

Paul gave a short nod, his breath heavy, sweat beading on his forehead. "Just about there—one more."

Together, they gritted their teeth and pulled again, and the wagon lurched free with a loud creak. The family let out a collective sigh as the wagon rolled out of the rut, wobbling on the uneven ground.

The father's knees nearly buckled as he rushed forward to clasp Paul's hand. "God bless you. My thanks—we would've been lost without you!"

Paul nodded, his eyes finding the horizon, where the last traces of sunlight were fading. "Glad we made it in time."

As the family worked to steady the wagon and collect themselves, Paul ran a hand over Dusty's coat, and she gave a soft snort, leaning in to snuffle his neck. Then, he glanced back at Eli, who wiped his brow with the back of his hand and met Paul's eyes with a quiet nod of acknowledgment.

The sun had all but disappeared by the time the family finished packing their things. The father was tightening the last of the ropes on the wagon when the mother approached, her hands clasped tightly in front of her.

"You ought to be careful," she murmured. "There were men up on that hill earlier. Watchin' us. They're gone now, but..."

Paul scanned the ridge for any sign of movement, then nodded, his jaw tight. "Smart to tell me. Get movin' and stay sharp."

She nodded, her hands trembling slightly as she turned back toward the wagon.

Paul's brow furrowed, his broad chest rising and falling slowly. They could've been rustlers, or maybe just drifters—either way, they were trouble. He pictured the terrain, the high ground, the blind spots where an ambush could come from.

He didn't expect those men to return before Paul and Eli made it back to camp, but he'd keep his hand near his gun anyway. They'd have to keep the herd close tonight, keep the men ready. If those bastards decided to move, Paul would make damn sure they didn't catch his men off guard.

Paul glanced at Eli, who'd gone pale, his gaze flicking nervously toward the hill. His fingers twitched at his side, as though itching for his gun.

"They gone?" Eli asked tightly.

Paul's eyes remained fixed on the ridge as he gave Dusty a final pat and mounted up. "For now."

Chapter Eight

Near Dover

Elsie hurried through the scrub. They'd been traveling for hours, and she desperately needed to relieve herself. She ducked into a patch of bushes, her heart thudding from the exertion of the day.

As she finished and straightened her clothes, footsteps behind her made her freeze. The hair on the back of her neck rose.

Before she could react, a rough hand grabbed her arm, spinning her around and shoving her to the ground. Rocks bit into her palms as she fell, losing her breath in a sharp gasp.

"I knew it." Bailey crouched beside her, his fingers tightening cruelly around her arm. A predatory smirk curled his lips.

Elsie tried to pull away, but his grip only tightened. "What do you want?"

"What do I want?" He tore at her shirt, exposing her breasts. "I *knew* you were hiding something. The others might be too stupid to see it, but not me."

Elsie's heart pounded as she struggled, but she couldn't move him.

"You're a woman." His dark laughter curled through the air like smoke as he leaned closer. "Figured it out a long time ago."

Elsie nearly gagged as the stench of Bailey's unwashed body overwhelmed her. "Get off me!"

"I could shout it right now. Tell the whole crew you've been lying to them."

Elsie's stomach dropped. He wouldn't. *Would he?*

"But I won't. Not if you do exactly what I say." He let go of her arm. "When we get to Wichita, you're gonna give me your pay. Every single dime."

Elsie's chest heaved, her pulse beating in her ears as she put on a show of bravado she didn't feel. "Why would I do that?"

Bailey's lips brushed her ear as he whispered, "If you don't, I'll make sure they know exactly what you are."

Her breath caught. She didn't have a choice. *If he tells the others, everything will be over.* The secret she'd fought so hard to protect would be out in the open, and she'd be ruined. Worse than ruined.

"Fine."

Bailey stood, brushing off his pants as if he hadn't just threatened her entire world. "That's a good girl."

He sauntered back toward the cattle.

Trembling, Elsie sat in the dust, her breath coming in sharp, uneven gasps. Her hands shook as she pulled her torn shirt back together, fumbling with the buttons. The world felt distant, the nearby sounds of cattle and men muffled by the roaring in her ears. Bailey's threat echoed in her head, louder than anything else.

She hugged her knees to her chest, curling in on herself. The future she'd fought so hard to build, her escape from Jon, the chance at a new life—it was all crumbling.

Jon's voice rang in her head, thick with whiskey, the door to her room slamming shut behind him. *"You think you can leave me, girl? You belong to me."*

Her hand tightened around the ragged edges of her shirt, the memory of his fingers bruising her skin as real as the dirt beneath her nails.

The first time she'd run, she'd slipped out in the dead of night, heart racing as she sprinted through the fields. He'd found her before she reached the road, dragging her back with a grip that promised pain, growling threats against her ear. Bailey's threat, his sneer—it was all too familiar; briefly, she felt the ghosts of chains wrap around her wrists.

Hot, unwanted tears blurred her vision as they welled up in her heavy-lidded eyes. She bit down hard on her lip, trying to force them back, but it was no use. The sobs came, ragged and uncontrollable, and her body shook with the effort of holding them in.

"I can't... I can't do this." She rocked slowly, trying to calm the panic clawing at her chest, but it only tightened around her ribs.

She hated how small and powerless she felt. Trapped. Without her pay, she wouldn't be able to run far enough to stay hidden from Jon. She was backed into a corner, and Bailey knew it.

Briefly, Paul's face flickered into her mind. She admired his quiet strength, the way he seemed to know right from wrong without batting an eye. *He knows what kind of man Bailey is.* He'd understand. But the idea of revealing the truth about herself, even to him, drove the breath from her lungs.

She couldn't do it.

Paul would look at her differently if he knew—maybe with pity, maybe with that flash of disgust she'd seen in Jon and his men. The thought twisted her stomach, made her want to crawl out of her own skin. She couldn't bear for him to see her like that, stripped down to nothing but the scared little girl Jon had tried to make her into.

"Come on, Elsie," she muttered under her breath. "You can't fall apart now. Not now."

Drawing in a deep, shuddering breath, she forced herself to stand.

Elsie's hands shook as she brushed her fingers against her arm, where Bailey had grabbed her. She straightened, trembling for only a moment before squaring her shoulders. She set her face as she wiped away the remnants of her tears, determination easing the pressure on her chest.

You'll survive this.

She couldn't let Bailey—or anyone else—break her.

With one final swipe at her face, she raised her chin and turned back toward camp.

The group was spread out, some resting, others tending the cattle or checking their gear. Paul stood near the edge of the camp, his stance calm but vigilant.

She could feel Bailey's eyes on her, though she refused to look at him. That smug smirk would still be on his face, like a predator that knew its prey was cornered.

She wouldn't let him see her weakness. She wouldn't give him that power.

Paul turned as she approached, his brow creasing. "You alright?"

"Fine. Just needed a moment."

"Storm's coming in," he muttered, seemingly to himself. "Best we get moving soon."

Elsie nodded, grateful for the shift in conversation. "I'll get our mounts ready."

She approached the horses, her heart pounding in her chest every time she felt Bailey's eyes on her. She made her steps deliberate, her movements steady. Internally, though, fear clawed at her, the humiliation still raw.

She worked quickly, tying ropes and checking saddles with mechanical precision. As she tightened the saddle straps, her mind shifted into the familiar rhythm of inventory.

Four days' worth of jerky left, maybe five if they rationed it right. The water barrels needed topping up, and she'd noticed one of the bridles fraying—another mile or two, and it'd snap clean through. She'd have to look for leather scraps when they reached Wichita, maybe trade one of her father's knives, if it came to that.

She'd always been good at keeping things together, even when everything else was falling apart.

Bailey lounged by the fire, but his eyes tracked her like a hawk trailing a mouse.

Elsie kept her head down, but her gaze darted to the shadows stretching across a narrow path leading toward the hills—an escape route, if she needed it. Every part of her screamed to be ready, to anticipate the moment when Bailey's grin turned into something deadlier.

She wouldn't be caught off guard again. *Not like with Jon.*

Bailey's voice cut through the quiet, low and mocking. "Everything alright, Eli?"

"Fine. Just getting the horses ready."

Bailey's chuckle grated against her ears. "Good. Wouldn't want anything slowin' us down."

Elsie finished securing the saddle and stepped away, wiping her hands on her trousers.

From the edge of camp, Paul called, "Move out!"

Elsie mounted quickly, avoiding Bailey's gaze as they headed out. She had to stay focused. She couldn't let anyone know what had happened.

As she rode, Marcus appeared at her side. "You alright, Eli?"

"Yeah," she replied quickly. *Too quickly.* She forced a nod, trying to make her voice sound steady. "Just needed a minute."

Marcus didn't respond right away. Even with only one good eye, his knowing gaze made her squirm—in fact, the cloudy film obscuring his other pupil somehow made his scrutiny even more unsettling. She kept her focus fixed ahead, refusing to look at him.

"You don't have to lie to me," he said finally. There was no accusation in his tone, just quiet concern. "I know when something's bothering someone."

Elsie's stomach twisted, and for a moment, she wondered if he'd figured it out—that she wasn't who she was pretending to be. The way he studied her... It was as if he could see right through the disguise she wore so carefully.

She shook her head. "Just got to get to Wichita. Then, I'll be done with it."

She'd heard stories about the city, about women who found work in saloons, sewing or cooking in the back. She could do that, even without the money from the trail run— slip into the shadows, cut her hair short, find a place where no one knew her name.

"You've got more to worry about than just getting to Wichita," Marcus muttered. "I've been around long enough to see when someone's carrying more than they can handle."

Elsie bit the inside of her cheek. *He knows. Maybe not everything, but enough.*

"You don't have to do it all on your own, Eli. Sometimes it helps to have someone else in your corner."

A lump rose in Elsie's throat. She wasn't used to anyone offering her help. Swallowing, she finally looked Marcus in the eye.

"I don't need anyone in my corner." The words were more reflex than truth.

He chuckled, a soft sound, almost lost in the pulse of hooves against the trail. "Maybe not. But if you ever change your mind, you know where I am."

Elsie didn't know how to respond. She gave a faint nod, feeling a slight weight lift off her, just enough to make the road ahead seem a little less daunting. She considered telling him everything, trusting him the way she'd trusted no one else.

She couldn't, though.

"Appreciate it, but once we're done here, I'll be gone. Easier that way."

Marcus nodded, his eyes lingering on her for a moment longer. "Alright. Just don't forget, the offer's there if you ever need it."

Elsie forced a small smile, though it felt hollow. "Thanks."

Chapter Nine

Near Dover

A gunshot cracked through the darkness.

Paul bolted upright, eyes straining in the black. Ignoring the cold leather biting into his skin, he shoved his boots on and snatched his rifle from the bedroll.

The cattle had gone wild, spooked by the gunfire, gentle lowing giving way to panicked bawling as the herd churned into a stampede.

Marcus's frantic shout pierced the night. "Paul! Paul, they're—"

A second shot, closer this time, cutting Marcus off.

Paul tore through the canvas flap, legs pumping, chest tight. The air stank of dust, sweat, and fear. Horses whinnied in panic, stamping nervously at the sudden noise and chaos. A wild-eyed steer was charging straight at Marcus, senseless with fear.

Paul managed to tackle Marcus out of the way just in time, sending them both tumbling. They hit the ground hard, the rough earth scraping Paul's hands raw, while nearby horses reared back, their nostrils flaring.

"Get clear," Paul roared, hauling Marcus up by his collar and shoving him toward the safety of the wagon. "Now!"

Marcus limped into the shadows without hesitation.

Paul's eyes swept the chaos, calculating what could go wrong.

The gully up ahead, the loose shale on the ridge—if the cattle hit either of those, they'd lose half the herd, maybe more. Fear turned these animals into a churning mass of muscle and terror. If he didn't turn the lead steer soon, the cattle would scatter into the dark, and come morning, Paul would be dragging carcasses out of the ravine.

Paul ran to Dusty. She shied back, nostrils flaring at the wild stampede, ears pinned flat against her head. Paul murmured soothingly as he leapt onto her back. She snorted when he yanked the reins, and he gave her a soft pat.

"Sorry, girl, but we gotta get in there." His breathing grew ragged as he forced the reluctant mare forward into the chaos.

He urged Dusty toward the front of the herd, mind already mapping out a path to lead the cattle back to safety. He spotted Eli as he stumbled out of his tent, pale and wide-eyed.

"Eli!" Paul bellowed. "Get mounted!" He didn't have time to check if the boy obeyed.

The herd surged like a living wave, bodies crashing together, hooves churning up clouds of dust that swallowed the camp in seconds. Paul's eyes darted around as he calculated distances, angles. The cattle's frantic bellowing mixed with the shouts of men, a cacophony that made thinking difficult.

The lead steer broke toward the supply wagon, nostrils flaring and eyes rolling in terror.

Dusty's reins were slick beneath Paul's fingers. The acrid scent of gunpowder and smoke from the campfire clung to the air as the steer balked, veering left, its massive body brushing past the wagon with inches to spare.

"Rocco! Jody!" Paul jumped to the ground and snatched a burning stick from the dying campfire. The heat scorched his fingers, but he didn't let go. "Don't let 'em scatter!"

Grit stuck to Paul's tongue and stung his eyes. Every breath burned with the sour tang of sweat. Dusty snorted disapprovingly, but didn't shy away when he approached. His fingers ached as he mounted again and gripped the reins, the burning stick scorching his skin as he swung it toward the fleeing shadows. The pounding of hooves vibrated through his legs, a reminder of how close they were to disaster.

Figures emerged from the shadows—Rocco's heavyset frame, Jody's lanky stride. They clutched torches, embers spitting as they sprinted to their horses. Muscles protesting, Paul kicked Dusty into a loping run. They plunged into the swirling dust, toward the cattle's bellows, deafening as thunder rolling across the plains.

A flash of movement—Paul snapped his rifle up. Dusty whinnied at the sudden motion, sidestepping as Paul clicked his tongue to steady her.

A rider darted past, swerving to avoid the stampede, and Paul fired. The man jerked and tumbled from his saddle. Paul's rifle cracked again, and another shadow dropped.

Before Paul could reload, a rustler rode toward him, his blade gleaming in the dim light.

Paul twisted, trying to swing his rifle as Dusty skittered sideways, spooked by the glint of the rustler's knife. She tossed her head, and Paul almost lost his balance. He gritted his teeth, tightening his legs to keep his seat, and jabbed the butt of his rifle into the man's jaw.

The rustler staggered but swung again, and Paul caught his wrist, twisting until he felt a snap. The man howled, dropping the blade, and Paul punched him and pushed him off his horse.

Paul shot the rustler and rushed back to Rocco and Jody.

Twin torches bobbed ahead, flickering against the darkness. They chased a shadowy figure deeper into the night, swallowed by the dust cloud. Paul kept his rifle ready and galloped to catch up to them.

"Keep up!" Paul called. "Don't lose sight of them!"

Eli pulled up beside Dusty Rose, panting. His mount was barely trained, dancing nervously beneath him with every gunshot. The boy's hands trembled on the reins, but he held his ground, trying to keep the animal steady.

"Keep close." Paul pushed a torch at Eli. "Don't let 'em split us."

Eli nodded, jaw clenched, and raised the torch high.

The ground dipped, and Paul yanked the reins, guiding Dusty over a gully that yawned like a black scar across the land. Rocco's horse stumbled, hooves skidding on scree, but Paul was already moving, eyes fixed on a shadowy figure ahead. Sagebrush whipped at his boots, and the scent of crushed leaves filled the air as their horses tore through the underbrush.

One misstep, and they'd be on the ground, trampled by their own mounts.

"Stay tight!" Paul said. "They're headin' for the creek!"

Another rustler rushed out of the dark on foot, eyes wild, pistol pointed up at Paul. Before Paul could react, Eli's pistol barked. The man staggered, collapsing into the dust.

Eli froze, his eyes fixed on the body.

Paul reached over, grabbing Eli's arm. "Eyes on me," he growled. "We ain't got time for that."

"They're splittin' up!" Rocco shouted, his torch bobbing as he veered left, after one of the fleeing rustlers.

"Jody, stick with him!" Paul barked, spurring Dusty forward.

He scanned the terrain, but the dust kicking up from the cattle made it hard to see. Another shadow darted through the swirling haze, and Paul cursed under his breath. They were circling back toward the wagons—toward the supplies.

If those bastards got to the food stores, it wouldn't just be the herd they lost—it'd be their water, their medicine, their only chance of making it through the next week without losing men.

The dust thickened, and for a moment, Paul couldn't see a damn thing. His gut told him to keep heading straight to the supplies, but the sound of pounding hooves to his right made him hesitate.

"Which way?" The faint glint of metal—a rustler's rifle—caught his eye, and he spurred Dusty toward it. "Eli, stay with me!"

Paul aimed, finger curling around the trigger, and fired. The rustler dropped with a grunt, his horse bolting into the night. The remaining rustlers peeled away, disappearing into the night like shadows.

They wouldn't be back—not after this—but the damage was done, the herd still spooked.

"Let 'em go," Paul ground out through clenched teeth. "We got bigger problems—Back to the herd!" He was already guiding Dusty Rose toward the scattered cattle. "Get 'em together before they bolt again!"

Paul dug his heels in, charging into the heart of the stampede. The cattle's eyes rolled white, but Paul didn't flinch.

He swung his rifle, smacking the lead steer's flank with the barrel. "Yah! *Yah!*"

The steer's hooves pounded the earth, sending rocks flying into the air, stinging Paul's face as he rode. Sweat dripped into his eyes, his muscles screaming with effort, but he didn't let up.

One wrong step, one miscalculation, and the massive animal would veer into him, sending him and Dusty crashing into the stampede. Paul swung his rifle again, smacking the barrel hard against the steer's flank. It let out a bellow, veering left just enough to nudge the rest of the herd back in line.

One by one, the cattle followed, their frenzied pace slowing as they recognized his voice, his commands. Sweat ran down Paul's back in rivers, but he kept moving, guiding the herd until the stampede became a stagger, then a shuffle, then—finally—stillness.

The last of the cattle settled, and Paul took stock.

Two head missing—likely trampled or bolted into the dark. Supplies scattered, one wagon listing to the side on a cracked wheel. He counted his men—Rocco, Jody, Marcus, Eli—all alive, but Marcus was favoring his leg, and Jody had a gash above his eyebrow.

"Rocco," Paul snapped, moving toward the nearest wagon. "Inventory check. Jody, you're on horses. Marcus, gather what you can—bandages, water, food. We've lost time, but we ain't lost the fight."

He glanced at Eli, who was staring into the darkness. "Eli, you're with me."

Paul led Eli back to the rustler he'd shot.

Eli slid off his saddle, stumbling over to where the body lay sprawled in a growing pool of blood. The boy had gone pale, shaking like a leaf in a storm. He stared down at the man, eyes distant, empty.

Paul remembered his own first kill: a Confederate boy barely older than Eli, crumpling at his feet in a field outside Chattanooga. His rifle had felt so heavy then, the blood staining his hands so red it took weeks to wash away. He'd never forgotten that face.

He knelt beside Eli, resting a calloused hand on his shoulder. "It don't get easy," he murmured. "You'll see him in your dreams. But you keep goin'. That's all there is." He squeezed Eli's shoulder. "One step at a time. Understand?"

Eli's hand drifted to his neck, fingers brushing over the old burns, and Paul felt the boy's shudder travel through him.

"He—when *he* had me…" Eli traced the angry red lines. "He'd… do this. For fun. I never wanted to be like him. Never wanted to hurt anyone."

Paul had seen that kind of cruelty before, in men who took pleasure in breaking what they thought was weaker. The kind who'd twist the knife, just to hear someone cry out. Eli's scars weren't just marks—they were reminders of a world that didn't care who it left bleeding.

The fact that he's so fair and feminine doesn't help either.

Inside, Paul's anger kindled. Not at Eli, but at a world that forced anyone—man or woman—to carry that kind of weight, that kind of pain. He understood it, in his own way. The world didn't give you a choice about the scars it left on you. All you could do was decide how to survive them.

"Sometimes, you don't get to choose. The world does it for you."

Eli nodded, lips trembling. "Makes it a bit easier, though. Havin' a reason."

"That it does."

Paul stood and took a step back, looking over the scattered camp. Something gnawed at him, a feeling he couldn't quite shake. Ragged breaths echoed in the silence, but it wasn't bruises or blood that worried him now.

I'm getting the Chickamauga feeling again.

The battle of Chickamauga had happened back in '63; they'd been marching through dense woodland, thinking the Confederate forces were still miles ahead. They hadn't seen it coming. Rebels had come out of nowhere, a silent ambush in the trees, and by the time shots fired, it was already too late.

Paul turned to check on the others, and that's when he saw Bailey, standing just beyond the circle of light, his eyes locked on Eli.

Something in his gaze sent a chill creeping up Paul's spine. It wasn't just anger or frustration. No, it was deeper than that—sharp and dangerous, like a knife in the dark. Paul had seen that look before, somewhere long ago, in a different fight.

But where…?

Bailey's lips curled into a smirk, and he turned away, disappearing into the shadows—but not before Paul caught his quiet, almost imperceptible whisper: "You ain't foolin' no one, kid."

Paul's jaw clenched; the words lingered in the air long after Bailey had vanished.

He had not seen Bailey in the battle.

Are you just a coward, or malicious?

"Come on," Paul muttered to Eli. "Let's get the camp sorted out."

But as they turned toward the dying fire, Paul couldn't shake the feeling that whatever storm had started brewing tonight was far from over—and that Bailey might be holding the thunder in his hands.

Chapter Ten

Near Enid

Every time Elsie glanced over her shoulder, Bailey was looking at her.

The way his scrutiny made her skin prickle reminded her of Jon. His threat hung over her, and it was exhausting. The idea that one simple sentence from him was enough to undo everything she was trying to achieve here. She fought to keep her hands steady as she packed a saddlebag.

She had no idea how the men would react if they discovered the truth.

Would Paul stand up for her, or would his loyalty to the rest of the crew come first? Would he see her as a liability, or as someone who had earned her place here? Rocco and Jody were even more of a mystery. Their rough demeanor and hardened attitudes offered no comfort, and she had no reason to believe they'd accept her deception lightly.

The thought of being cast out, left alone in the wilderness with nothing but the clothes on her back, twisted her insides in knots. She didn't know if she'd survive it—not out here, not with Jon looming somewhere beyond the horizon.

Still, she wouldn't give Bailey the satisfaction of seeing the fear on her face.

A sense of loss all hung over the camp. Marcus's tent was gone, lost in last night's skirmish, and the damage wasn't limited to supplies. One of the mares had a nasty gash on her flank. The rest of the animals, horses and cattle, were restless, shifting, stomping, and flicking their ears.

They packed up in silence, expressions hard and weary.

Marcus kept glaring at the empty spot where his tent had stood, muttering under his breath as he tightened the cinch on his saddle. Rocco kicked at the dirt, his frustration barely contained, while Jody's characteristic energy had deserted him. No one spoke, and when they finally mounted up and rode out, there was none of the usual banter, no complaints—just the creak of leather and the rhythmic clop of hooves against the dry earth.

There wasn't much to say, really. Not after the night they'd had.

Elsie kept to the back of the group, her eyes scanning the horizon. She'd just started to relax her shoulders, trying to ease the tension that had settled there, when Paul dropped back to ride alongside her. His presence was a welcome distraction, and for a moment, she almost forgot about the watchful eyes following her every move.

"Say, Eli, what's your plan after this?" Paul asked casually, as if they weren't riding through a harsh and unforgiving landscape, as if they weren't all on edge.

Elsie tightened her grip on the reins. She hadn't thought that far ahead. The money she'd hoped to earn at the end of this drive had been her ticket to a life away from Jon. Now, with Bailey breathing down her neck, the future felt more uncertain than ever. Jon's specter—his threats, his control, his punishments—loomed over her.

Then again, even if she somehow managed to keep the money, she wasn't sure she could actually escape Jon forever.

He always found me before.

He knew her too well, knew where to look, how to track her down. Her chest tightened, and she forced herself to take a breath.

"I... I don't really have a plan." The words tasted strange as they left her mouth. She wasn't used to admitting she didn't know something. "Figured I'd go wherever the wind takes me."

"You're good with cattle. You could do something with that."

Unexpected warmth bloomed in Elsie's chest. It had been so long since anyone recognized her skills—since anyone had seen her as capable of something other than just surviving. Not since her father. The reminder of everything he'd taught her brought a bittersweet ache to her heart.

She straightened in her saddle. "My pa taught me everything I know."

"That right?"

She remembered her father's strong, calloused hands showing her how to tie knots, his voice patient as he guided her small fingers through each loop and pull. *A good knot, Elsie, is like a promise—hard to break if you do it right.* He'd told her. She could hear his laughter, deep and full, echoing across the ranch when she'd managed to get it right the first time. The pride in his eyes had made her feel ten feet tall.

"He was a real cowboy, through and through." She smiled. "Used to say that the only way to really understand cattle was to think like 'em. He could read a herd like nobody else. Knew their mood just by looking at 'em."

"Sounds like he had a real gift."

"He taught me to respect 'em, to see them as more than just dumb animals. Some folks thought he was one brick shy of a full load, talking to cattle like they were people, but they trusted him." *I trusted him, too.* "I remember being just a little thing, standing on the fence while he worked, and he'd call me over, put a rope in my hands, and tell me to try."

Her father had done more than let her try. They'd camp by the cattle—just the two of them, out under the stars, the night sky wide and clear above them—watching for trouble from predators or otherwise. He'd make a fire and tell her stories about places he'd seen and people he'd met. When he spoke of danger, of violent storms and ruthless rustlers, he'd drop his voice to an ominous whisper, but he'd always ended his stories with a smile.

Paul's voice brought her back to the present. "Did you? Try, I mean?"

Elsie chuckled, her eyes brightening. "Every time. He always said—"

She stopped herself just in time, the words dying in her throat. Her father had always said, *"My little girl could out-rope any man in Texas!"*

She cleared her throat, shifting awkwardly in the saddle. "He said cattle were smarter than people give 'em credit for."

Paul gave her a curious look.

"What about you?" she asked, trying to deflect his piercing gaze. "What's your plan?"

"I got a ranch." He sighed. "Lot's o' work to be done on it. Fences need fixing, barn's falling apart, fields lying fallow. Supposed to be something worth doing, I guess."

As he spoke, she noticed a distance in his tone—like he was describing a place he had no real connection to, as though his ranch had lost its shine somewhere along the way. She felt hesitant to ask him about it, though.

Sure wouldn't like someone poking their nose into my past.

Before she could decide, both their heads snapped up at a commotion up ahead.

Bailey, who'd been riding at the front, swayed and tumbled from his saddle, his horse skittering to the side in surprise. He ended up on his hands and knees, retching violently.

Rocco and Jody exchanged glances but made no move to help.

Paul sighed, pressing his lips together as he spurred Dusty Rose forward. Elsie followed him with narrowed eyes, watching Bailey.

His face was flushed, his hands shaking as he struggled to get back to his feet. *This isn't just the results of a bad meal.* From the way his glassy eyes darted around, as if he couldn't make sense of his surroundings, something was obviously very wrong.

Jon had been like that once—eyes wild, his face twisted in a mixture of rage and fear. He'd been drinking for days, his temper growing shorter with every passing hour. She'd tried to avoid him, to stay out of his way, but it hadn't mattered. He'd found her in the barn, his voice slurred as he accused her of things that made no sense, things she hadn't done.

She doubted Bailey was just drunk, though.

Paul dismounted and reached for Bailey's hand.

"I'm fine." Bailey jerked his arm away. "Just leave me be!"

The bout of vomit that followed called those words into question, though.

"We need to stop." Elsie reined in her horse next to them. "He's not well."

Bailey let out a harsh bark of laughter, his eyes wild as he glared up at her. "Ain't none of your business, *Eli*."

Elsie frowned. Whatever was working its way through Bailey was affecting his mind, which made him dangerous. Bailey's gun was at his hip, within easy reach; in a moment of delirium, he might shoot any of them.

Worse, he might spill her secret, regardless of the money she'd promised him.

"Paul." She made her voice firm. "We have to *stop*."

Paul hesitated, glancing between her and Bailey, then nodded. "Alright." He pointed to a shaded area off the trail. "We'll set up over there. Rocco, Jody—help me move him."

Crossing his arms, Rocco frowned. "Why should we? Guy's been nothing but trouble."

"Yeah, Paul. He'll be fine on his own." Jody rolled his eyes. "Probably just bent his elbow too far and needs to sleep it off."

"We can't just leave him. He's one of us, like it or not."

Rocco sighed dramatically. "Fine—but don't expect me to stick around if he starts swingin'."

Jody shook his head. "Let's just get it over with."

Paul turned back to Bailey. "C'mon, Bailey. Work with us here."

Rocco and Jody exchanged another glance before dismounting reluctantly. They grabbed Bailey by the arms, their expressions filled with disdain as they lifted him. Bailey stumbled, nearly collapsing into them, and they recoiled visibly.

Elsie followed behind them.

"He's heavier than he looks," Jody grumbled, grimacing. "Feels like dead weight."

Rocco's lip curled as he struggled to keep his grip. "Yeah, well, maybe if he hadn't drunk whatever swamp water he'd found, we wouldn't be stuck doing this."

Paul rolled his eyes. "Just get him over there. The sooner we settle, the sooner we can all rest."

He led them toward the shaded area, his own movements quick and efficient, but the irritation was clear in every step.

"You know, this ain't what I signed up for." Rocco grumbled under his breath. "Playing nursemaid to some idiot who can't take care of himself."

Jody sighed wearily. "Yet here we are. Figures."

Paul shot them a sharp look. "Enough."

Finally, the unwilling pair set Bailey down with a grunt. They stood back, wiping their hands on their trousers as if ridding themselves of something foul as Bailey groaned and slumped over.

"There. Done," Rocco muttered with a shake of his head.

Elsie knelt beside Bailey and touched his forehead gingerly. *He's burning up.* "I need water, strips of cloth, and my bag of herbs."

"Think you can... hide..." Bailey mumbled, his head lolling. "*Can't* hide... Can't lie... Can't..."

Elsie stiffened, her heart pounding.

Don't say it.

She held her breath, but Bailey's words slipped into incoherence. His eyes rolled back, and his body sagged, unconscious.

Mouth suddenly dry, Elsie swallowed hard.

That was close—too close.

Chapter Eleven

Near Enid

Bailey was getting worse.

Two days had passed since the first signs of illness, and now he couldn't even keep water down. The sallow tone of his skin had grown even more pronounced, and his eyes were sunken, framed by dark circles. He'd cough weakly between bouts of vomiting, the stench of sickness mingling with the sour aroma of weeks—maybe months—without bathing. He trembled constantly, his hands twitching. He screamed in the night.

Paul had seen his share of illness in the war, but something about this felt different. More hopeless. It made him feel like death himself stood just beyond the firelight, biding his time.

Paul stood at the edge of the camp, arms crossed, scanning the horizon as sunlight crept over the dry landscape.

Rocco approached him. "We gotta leave him, Paul. Look at 'im—he's already halfway to the grave."

Rocco's weathered face was set in a hard scowl, the expression only deepening the lines of his leathery skin. His hands flexed at his sides.

Paul's jaw tightened. He didn't like Bailey, not one bit. The man had always been difficult—stubborn and abrasive—the kind of man who was easy to dislike. A few times, Paul had considered just sending him away, Aldo be damned.

But the thought of abandoning him here to die alone, didn't sit right. There was a line that Paul wouldn't cross, no matter how much a man wronged him.

Rubbing the back of his neck, Jody followed behind Rocco. "Dragging him along could kill us all, Paul. If the sickness spreads...."

Jody had a point, but that didn't make the decision any easier.

It had been the same back in Chattanooga in '63, when fever had spread through the camp like wildfire. Paul had watched as strong men were reduced to hollow shells, barely clinging to life. The doctor's tent had born the acrid smell of sickness, mixed with the metallic tang of blood and the cries of men whose bodies had betrayed them.

Yet, they'd never abandoned any of them.

There was Jeremiah, a boy no older than Eli, whose face had turned gray before he breathed his last. Thomas, who'd begged Paul to write a letter to his mother, the request barely audible over the rattle of his breath.

"We don't leave our own," Paul said finally, his voice low but firm. Rocco and Jody exchanged glances, but Paul didn't give them room to argue. "We wait."

Paul could do so much to protect the group—fend off predators, keep raiders at bay, navigate through harsh weather—but illness was something he couldn't fight.

He hated that feeling of powerlessness, like he was trying to hold back a flood with his bare hands.

As the hours passed and the sun dipped lower in the sky, Paul remained at his post, his thoughts churning. Shadows had stretched long, painting the camp in somber light, when Eli approached slowly, his face pale. His shoulders drooped like he was burdened with a great weight. The resignation in Eli's expression made Paul's stomach twist—the look of a man who'd seen the limits of his own ability and come up short.

The dark circled beneath his bloodshot eyes reminded Paul of Little Sammy, a boy from his unit back in the war. Sammy had always tried to be brave, to keep up and hide his fear even as the reality of war bore down on him. Paul could still remember the night Samuel had finally broken down, trembling in exhaustion and sobbing quietly in the dark when he thought no one could hear.

Sammy had never really recovered.

Paul gulped. He could not, *would* not, let Eli's eyes turn hollow like Little Sammy's had.

"Paul..." Eli called softly, the late afternoon breeze stealing his words away.

"He's almost gone, isn't he?"

Eli nodded, rubbing at his face. "It's... it's bad, Paul. I think it's cholera. I don't think he's been boiling his water."

"Some things, you just can't stop, Eli." Paul tried to sound reassuring, but the words felt clumsy in his mouth.

"I just... I don't know what else to do. It feels like no matter how hard I try, it's not enough." Eli looked down, his shoulders shaking. " I feel like it's my fault."

Frustration and hopelessness poured out of the boy. Eli was an emotional man, and Paul had no idea how to respond properly.

"You did all you could. Sometimes..." Paul stepped closer and placed an awkward hand on Eli's shoulder. "Sometimes, that's all we can do."

The sentiment felt empty, but it was true. Out here, all you could do was try—even when you knew it wouldn't be enough.

Eli sniffed, wiping at his face as his chest rose and fell in jagged motions. Eventually, his tired eyes began to regain some focus, and he took a deep breath, drawing himself up.

It was a small gesture, but it spoke of determination—a reminder of the strength Paul had seen in Eli time and time again. He wanted to do more, to offer the boy some comfort, but...

What else can I say?

Before Paul could figure it out, Marcus approached. He nodded at Paul and put a hand on Eli's back. "C'mon, son. Let's get this done."

They walked back together, the sounds of Bailey's suffering intensifying as they approached. Bailey sprawled on his bedroll, panting and damp with sweat.

Paul knelt beside him, watching as his breathing grew more labored, each gasp more desperate than the last.

Eli just stood there.

Bailey let out one last, rattled breath—and then went still.

The silence that followed was thick, heavy. It pressed down, wrapping around the camp like a shroud. Paul looked at Eli.

The boy almost seemed relieved.

That's odd.

Bailey was a nasty piece of work, sure, but Paul didn't see a reason for anyone to be relieved by his death. Then again...

Eli had been awfully skittish around the man, using every opportunity to avoid him.

Paul shook his head. He had more important things to worry about. If the boy wanted to confide in him, he would.

He looked at Rocco and Jody. "We'll build a cairn. Make sure the scavengers don't get to him."

Rocco opened his mouth, but Paul glared at him. Rocco turned on his heel and shuffled off toward the creek bed, grumbling under his breath.

Jody followed, dragging his feet like a kid asked to do chores. His reddish hair, tousled and wild, gleamed with sweat as he trudged behind Rocco.

To contemplate leavin' a man's corpse like spoiled meat... Shameful.

Paul reached out and closed Bailey's eyes.

He'd gotten used to the man's moaning and groaning over the past few days; now, without it, the quiet felt louder.

Death had that way about it.

Rocco and Jody returned, arms laden with rocks from the creek. Paul joined them, piling the smooth stones on the body. The sound of stone against earth filled the space where Bailey's breathing used to be. Paul worked slowly, deliberately, placing each rock carefully, like it mattered.

It does, no matter what they think.

Leaving Bailey behind would've been easy, but *easy* didn't sit right with Paul. The body would draw predators. Worse, sickness could spread if they weren't careful. Besides, Bailey—for all his faults—was a human being; he deserved to be laid to rest respectfully.

As the last stone settled into place, they stepped back. The cairn was rough and uneven, and probably wouldn't last long before weather or wildlife uncovered what lay beneath. They'd had no time to dig an actual grave, but at least they'd done something.

Paul stood at the edge of the monument, his head bowed slightly. His jaw felt tight, and his shoulders slumped momentarily before he squared them again and turned to face the others.

"Mount up. We're done here."

***

Paul waited until they'd set up camp to approach Eli.

"We'll reach a trading post in a few days," he murmured as he sat by the campfire beside Eli. "Aldo needs to know what happened. I'll send word."

"Alright."

"You gonna tell me what's eatin' you, or are we just gonna keep pretending you're fine?"

"It's nothin'." Eli's fingers twitched, but he didn't look up. The kid sat like stone, staring into the fire as if it might burn away whatever was clawing at him. "Ain't worth talkin' about."

"Ain't nothin'."

Eli let out a shaky breath that carried a thousand unspoken words. His shoulders hunched forward, and Paul could see his exhaustion—not just from the trail, but something deeper, something festering.

"I get it," Paul whispered. "We all got things we keep buried. But out here, you let it eat at you, it'll tear you apart. Seen it too many times."

"What do you want from me, Paul?" Eli's eyes flicked up, and Paul saw it again—rawness, desperation—before the kid looked away, burying it under that mask he always wore. "You think I ain't tryin' to hold it together?"

"I think you've been tryin' too hard, and it's breakin' you down."

"You wouldn't understand."

"Try me."

"Bailey..." For a moment, Eli didn't move, didn't breathe. "I..."

"What about Bailey?"

Eli stared into the fire, flames dancing in his eyes, before he finally whispered, "I couldn't stand him. *Hated* him. When he got sick, when he died... part of me was glad."

"Ain't wrong to feel that way. Man like Bailey earn more enemies than friends. But that's not what's really been eatin' at you, is it?"

"I thought I was better than that."

"Ain't about that, kid. You did what you had to. We all did."

Eli's eyes closed, his shoulders finally relaxing. The fire crackled, but the silence that followed felt easy, the kind of quiet that settled things.

"We'll keep movin' forward," Paul rose and brushed the dirt from his pants. "Ain't no other way."

Eli remained, staring at the fire.

The wind picked up, carrying the scent of sagebrush and dust, and something else—something sharp and metallic that set Paul's teeth on edge. He glanced up at the stars, barely beginning to blink into existence, and a knot formed in his chest.

He had a bad feeling. He didn't understand why, especially since Bailey was dead.

I just hope it has nothing to do with Eli.

Chapter Twelve

Near Pond Creek

The storm rolled in faster than Paul had expected.

Dark clouds gathered above, wind whipping through the grasses, driving the herd forward with growing panic. Ahead, a ravine cut sharply across their path, and the sheer drop of a jagged cliff loomed beyond it, visible through the haze of dust and rain.

One wrong move, and the herd would plummet into the abyss.

He'd seen it before out here—storms brewing fast, like nature itself was in a hurry to tear everything apart. At times, you got no warning, no sign, until the weather was right on top of you. When the storm was coming, the only choice was to prepare for the worst and hope for something better.

However, hope didn't stop cattle from stampeding, leaping headlong off cliffs or getting trampled under their own kind. Only good judgment and experience could keep a herd together, and when that failed, you counted your losses and moved on.

"Keep 'em tight," Paul barked at Rocco.

The cattle shifted nervously, kicking up dirt and grass. The storm was upon them, but there was nothing to do but ride it out.

Everything seemed under control for the moment.

Then, the first crack of lightning split the sky, seeming to hit the ground just feet away.

A deafening crack reverberated through the air, and the herd exploded into chaos. Cattle scattered in every direction, wild eyes rolling in fear.

Damn it!

It only took a flash, a rumble, and all control was gone. Inevitably, the animals' instinct to run proved stronger than anything else. The challenge now wasn't stopping the stampede but steering it—directing all that fear away from the ravine and toward safety. It wasn't about winning; it was about surviving.

Paul kicked Dusty into motion, and she charged toward the front of the herd.

He rose above the chaos, keeping Dusty steady as the cattle bolted with a confidence born from years on the trail. Reaching out, he caught the reins of a stray horse, pulling it back into line.

The rain was coming down in sheets now, but he focused on one thing—steering the herd away from the cliff. Every second counted. Every decision could mean the difference between surviving this storm and losing half their stock.

Everything else blurred into the background. When you lost control, stampedes ended in broken legs and snapped necks more often than not. Paul had made a promise to Aldo, and the men were counting on him to keep it.

He nudged Dusty closer to the lead steer, pushing him to veer away, praying the herd would follow.

Eli was already there, racing ahead, weaving through the frightened cattle.

Paul found himself impressed with how the kid moved, how he managed to stay calm in the middle of the storm. Paul had seen men twice Eli's age break under this kind of pressure, but Eli didn't falter. He drove the cattle back, keeping them tight, and in that moment, Paul glimpsed something more than just a kid trying to survive the trail. He had grit, the kind that couldn't be taught, only earned.

Paul stored that thought away, an ember of respect growing for the boy who refused to back down.

Another flash of lightning—closer this time. Not far from the herd, a towering tree exploded in a shower of sparks and splinters. A dozen cows panicked, pressing toward the ragged cliff.

Paul's stomach lurched. *We can't stop them in time.*

"Get back!" Paul shouted, spurring Dusty forward through the madness. He pushed toward the edge of the ravine, but it was too late—several cows dove over, disappearing into the abyss below.

Paul pulled Dusty to a stop, breathing hard as the pounding rain soaked through his coat. He turned toward the ravine and peered over the edge. Far below, ten cattle lay dead or dying, twisted and broken on the jagged rocks.

He cursed under his breath, but there was nothing to be done for them now.

Seeing the dead never got easier, even when they were just cattle. He'd been on drives where a man counted every loss against his paycheck, each animal another nail in his coffin. Paul understood that, but he'd learned a long time ago not to mourn what couldn't be changed. The trail took what it wanted, and today it'd claimed ten head. It could've been more, and that was the closest thing to mercy the trail ever gave.

Paul glanced down one last time, mentally tallying the count, then forced himself to move on.

Dwelling on the dead's a quick way to join 'em.

Back in the war, they hadn't always had time to bury the dead or save the wounded. The men who tried often ended up with a bullet in their back or caught in the next shell blast. He'd lost count of the abandoned bodies, men he'd fought alongside; their faces emerged, fresh in his memory, even now.

It wasn't death that scared Paul; it was how swiftly it could claim everything you worked for.

After the war, he'd sworn he'd never be caught off guard again. Survival had become a way of life. He didn't have the luxury of mourning for the scorched earth, the people left picking up the pieces—not if he wanted to keep the others alive.

Eli rode up beside him, breathing hard, rain dripping from his hat. His face was pale, but his eyes focused steadily on the scene below.

"Aldo's gonna be fit to be tied."

"Aldo always factors some losses into every drive." Paul shook his head. "Ten head won't break him."

Aldo didn't expect miracles—just results. Cattle were valuable, but they weren't people. They could be replaced, bought, bartered for. Aldo knew that. Hell, *Paul* knew that. What Aldo wouldn't stand for was weakness. That's why Paul was leading this drive—Aldo trusted him not to bend, no matter what the trail threw at him.

"Still feels like a waste," Eli muttered.

"The trail don't give a damn. If it ain't the storm, it's something else."

Eli's brow furrowed. "Still—ten head? That's a lot, Paul."

"Trust me. Aldo's been in this business long enough to know the risks."

"Maybe. Don't make it easier."

When Paul looked the kid, rain mixing with the sweat and mud on his lean body, something about his presence on the drive made sense.

Eli had something most men didn't—an understanding of what had to be done, if reluctantly, even when it came down to making hard decisions. Paul had seen hints of it before, but his actions today had cemented it. You didn't stay calm in the middle of a storm like this without something deeper. Leadership wasn't just about calling shots; it involved holding your nerve when the world went sideways.

Eli had that.

"You think you're the first to woe the losses?" Paul smiled and patted the kid's shoulder. "You did good out there today. Kept your head."

Eli's cheeks grew red, his mouth opening like he had more to say, but no words came. After a moment, he settled with a small nod. "Still doesn't feel right. I keep thinkin' we could've done more."

"You spend your life thinkin' that way, it'll eat you alive. Only so much you can do. The rest is up to the trail."

"Guess I'm still learning that."

Paul watched him a second longer. "Get some rest. We'll be movin' again soon."

That was that kind of cold pragmatism that had earned Paul a reputation among the men. He knew how to cut losses, how to let things go. He'd rebuilt his life after the war, brick by brick, taking whatever work he could get, learning to lead by observing experienced men. That was why he'd taken up cattle drives—he liked the challenge of keeping the herd intact and the men focused, all while facing down storms, rustlers, and worse.

Well, that, and to escape the ghosts that haunted his empty ranch.

Jody came limping up with a fresh scrape across his cheek, globs of muck oozing down the leather of his chaps.

Paul raised an eyebrow. "Take a tumble?"

"Horse got spooked." Jody spat on the ground, wincing. "Didn't see it comin'."

Eli rushed up to Jody and examined him with a practiced eye and gentle hand. The delicate way he touched the scratch on Jody's cheek, the softness of his tone...

He's so... feminine.

Patting Jody's arm, Eli stepped back. "You'll be alright." He looked up at Paul. "He just needs to sit a spell."

Paul nodded as Eli helped Jody onto a nearby rock. "Storm rattled all of us. Just keep a tighter grip next time."

Jody glowered at him. "I ain't no greenhorn, Paul."

Eli grinned. "Could've fooled me, hard as you hit the ground!"

"You think you coulda stayed on?"

"Guess we'll never know." Eli chuckled. "I keep my horse calmer than yours."

"You don't want me callin' you a greenhorn, you stop actin' like one." Paul crossed his arms. "We can't afford anyone else takin' a spill. You keep your eyes on the trail, not the sky."

Jody grumbled under his breath, but Paul let it slide. The man was more bark than bite, but after a fall like that, he'd be bruised in more ways than one.

"We'll camp here," Paul called to Rocco, who was already gathering up the gear. "Let the storm pass before we move again."

Rocco grunted, dragging their supplies toward a small stand of trees that would offer some shelter from the storm. The wind still howled, but the worst of it seemed to have moved on; the rain tapered off into a steady drizzle as Marcus guided the remaining cattle toward the makeshift camp.

Paul approached Marcus, who was focused on the herd. "How many injured?"

Marcus didn't look up. "Five or six might've turned a leg, but they should be fine once they settle."

"Good. Don't need more losses on top of the ten that went over."

"Ain't our first storm, and it won't be the last." Looking up, Marcus's one good eye finally met Paul's. "Long as the rest of the herd's sound, we'll manage."

"Eli held his own out there," Paul remarked after a beat.

Marcus followed Paul's gaze to Eli, who was helping Jody rid his clothes of mud. "That one's tougher than he looks."

"Sure enough," Paul murmured.

Thunder rumbled in the distance, but for now, the cluster of trees offered them a quiet reprieve. The herd was calming, and the men, tired and shaken as they were, had made it through in one piece. Paul cast one more look toward the ravine before turning his eyes to the road ahead.

The trail wasn't done with them yet.

Chapter Thirteen

Near Pond Creek

The cattle drifted toward a patch of green ahead like ducks after a June bug. Paul watched them go, but his mind was a thousand miles away.

Though he'd never been the type to dream big, his ranch had once been the exception. He'd pictured a whitewashed house, large barn, fields of golden grain stretching out beyond the fence line, and... *her* lilting tones calling to him from the porch. That sweet voice had carried him through the war, the trails, and every hard winter that'd threatened to break him.

But now, with every mile behind him, the memory of that voice grew softer and harder to reach.

Despite what Katherine had done to him, he feared the day it would vanish entirely, leaving him with nothing but silence.

He barely registered Eli's offer to corral the cattle, stuck in thoughts that had been gnawing at him for days.

The future.

It loomed like the open prairie, vast and uncertain. The Chisholm Trail had been his lifeline, but as the railroads expanded, everything was changing. Trail runs were shutting down faster than the spread of small-town gossip.

He'd have to start thinking about his ranch again. Fixing it up, running it, living there alone.

Always with the memory of *her.*

The ranch was supposed to have been *their* dream, not just his. With every nail he'd driven, every fence post he'd sunk into the earth, her laughter had been in his ears. The idea of finishing the work alone twisted him all up, just a reminder that no matter how far he rode, how many trails he took, he'd never be able to outrun what he'd lost.

A shout broke through his thoughts, and his head snapped up, swiveling to find the source of the commotion.

His eyes lit on Eli, who was darting between cattle, a figure on horseback bearing down on him.

Paul's heart jolted, and for a split second, he was back in the war, the smell of gunpowder thick in the air, the weight of life and death hanging on the pull of a trigger. Shaking himself, he spurred Dusty forward, and everything narrowed to that rider, the threat closing in on Eli. Paul wasn't about to let another life slip through his fingers. Not today.

Not Eli.

The rider was close, though, and faster than Eli's horse could manage. Paul gripped the reins tightly as Dusty galloped across the rough terrain. His body moved with her rhythm, every muscle working in tandem. The wind tugged at the brim of his Stetson, and he set his jaw, hardening his face into a mask of focus as the landscape blurred past.

Faster, kid, faster!

Eli's horse stumbled on a patch of scree, and his pursuer surged forward, leaning over, his arm stretching out, fingers poised to grab the back of Eli's shirt.

"Move, damn it!" Paul bellowed, urging Dusty to go faster.

Eli jerked to the side, twisting in the saddle, and his pursuer's hand grasped empty air.

The attacker snarled, falling back just long enough to regain his balance. He snatched a lasso from his saddle and swung the loop in a wide arc before launching it forward. The loop snapped through the air and fell around Eli's shoulders, then tightened with a brutal yank.

No!

Eli's horse bucked in terror and reared up on its hind legs. Eli grabbed the rope with both hands and fought against the pull, struggling to stay in the saddle as his attacker yanked him closer, hauling him in like a fish.

Come on, kid!

Paul reached for his own rope, rushing to form a loop, when a blinding glint caught his eye. Eli's hand had flashed to the knife at his belt, and in one swift motion, he slashed the rope, the severed end whipping through the air.

The strange rider lurched backward in his saddle as the rope went slack.

In that brief second, Eli kicked his horse forward and tore away from the attacker, who regrouped, spewing curses, and sprinted after him.

"Eli—left!" Paul hollered.

As Eli veered sharply, the attacker swung his lasso again. This time, he aimed lower and caught Eli's horse around the neck. The animal jerked violently and stumbled as the rope pulled taut.

Paul didn't hesitate. He drove Dusty straight at the bastard, their horses nearly colliding, and walloped him square in the face. The man's grip slipped, the rope slipping from his hands, and Paul followed up with a punch to his ribs, feeling the crack of bone beneath his knuckles.

A bullet whistled through the air, and the attacker cursed and jerked his horse to the side.

Paul spun around, searching for the source of the shot, and saw Marcus up on a ridge, smoke curling from the barrel of his weapon.

The strange rider snarled, then turned his attention back to Eli. "You better run hard and far, little bird! He's coming!" With that, he turned tail and fled like double-struck lightning.

Paul tugged on the reins to slow Dusty Rose, staring after him. That man hadn't just been some greenhorn out for a joyride. He'd had a look about him, the look of a man who knew how to break a spirit before breaking a body.

That man would share a plate with a rattler, then eat the snake for dessert.

What men like that left behind was never pretty. Burned-out homesteads, families left with nothing but graves to tend. Paul had buried enough friends to know that kind of cruelty didn't just take lives—it took everything worth living for. That man wouldn't have hesitated to gut them all if it meant getting to Eli.

The thought stirred something fierce inside Paul.

He rode up to Eli and put his hand on the kid's shoulder just as Rocco and Jody caught up.

"Easy, kid," Paul murmured. "Ain't no shame in bein' rattled. Seen grown men with a lot less reason to chew the bit."

Eli didn't answer right away, but his eyes stayed on Paul's, as if weighing the words.

Paul considered how young Eli was, yet carrying burdens that would crush the most hardened men. Just like boys who'd taken up arms too early, their eyes already hollowed out by the weight of a world that expected too much. Eli wore that same look sometimes, though he obviously tried to hide it.

"Didn't think you'd come face-to-face with that gang leader of yours today, did you?"

"Wasn't him. Just one of his men." Eli shook his head. "I thought I had more time. Thought maybe I'd lost 'em back in Oklahoma. Should've known better."

"You can't predict what a man like that'll do. You just deal with him when he shows up."

Eli gulped. He had the look of prey that'd caught a whiff of a predator closing in. Paul's chest tightened with a knot of pity that had no place out here on the trail.

Paul glanced up as Marcus rode in, rifle still resting across his lap, then at Rocco.

"Who was that?" Rocco looked back and forth between them.

"Layton." Eli swallowed. "His name is Layton. He works with the man who's been lookin' for me—his right-hand man."

Paul's gut churned. He wouldn't even consider leaving Eli to his own fate as an option, even if it might save them some trouble. Of course, the gang leader might've been the vindictive type who'd come after them regardless. It didn't matter either way. Paul wouldn't leave a man like *Bailey* behind, let alone *Eli*.

Marcus leaned forward. "What's this about, Eli?"

"I'd hoped I'd never have to tell anyone." Eli exhaled slowly. "Figured if I just kept movin', I could outrun him. But Layton... he's like a bloodhound. He always seems to know where to find me."

Paul frowned. "So, the leader doesn't do the trackin' himself?"

Eli scoffed. "He never does *anything* himself."

Marcus pursed his lips. "What's this about a gang leader, now?"

"I used to live on a farm with my pa." Eli stared into the dirt. "Then, Jonathan Rickett showed up askin' for money. Pa pushed back, and that's when things got ugly. Pa's gone now, and Rickett's been after me for... what I took from him."

"Jonathan Rickett," Marcus tested the name like a snake's rattle in his mouth. "Heard of him. Man's been burnin' his way through Oklahoma, leaving bodies wherever he can't get his way. Ain't a small fish you're runnin' from, Eli."

Rocco spat into the dirt as Jody gaped. "And you brought him on us?"

"I didn't ask for this," Eli whispered. "Didn't ask for him to chase me across three states."

"Might be easier if you'd just keep ridin'." Rocco shook his head. "Saved us some trouble."

Paul scowled. "And what then? You'd sleep easy knowin' you left a kid out here to fend for himself?"

"I ain't sayin' it's right, just sayin'... It'd be simpler."

"Nothin's ever simple, Jody." Marcus shot Rocco a hard look. "Not out here."

"What'd you take from him?" Rocco asked.

"Myself." Eli shook his head. "He's hellbent on gettin' me back."

Jody, who'd been quiet in the back, swore under his breath. Rocco just stared, his mouth twisted like he'd just swallowed a mama hornet. They'd signed up for a cattle drive, not a blood feud with a ruthless outlaw.

"Eli, are we lookin' at a pack of dogs, or an army?" Marcus shifted in his saddle. "Rickett's got a reputation for pulling in men as mean as he is. If they come for you, we need to know how bad it's gonna get."

"Just a pack," Eli replied, "but they're loyal to Rickett, and that makes 'em dangerous. Men like Layton—they ain't in it for the money. They're in it 'cause Rickett offers 'em power over whoever crosses their path."

"Don't you worry." Marcus patted his rifle. "We'll get you to Wichita and get the law involved. Rickett ain't gonna to touch you."

"No man ought to live scared." Paul met Eli's eyes. "You're with us."

Paul believed Rocco and Jody would make the right call. That they wouldn't step back and ignore Eli's plight as they had with Bailey. The kid was stout, dependable, always willing to help, and his knowledge of plant lore had come in handy more times than one.

And he's got a good heart. That's got to count for somethin'.

"Wichita ain't much safer if he's got men sniffin' around," Rocco muttered, but his voice had lost its edge.

"Rickett ain't the first outlaw we've faced, and he won't be the last," Paul declared, "but we'll make him regret comin' after one of ours."

Jody shuffled his feet, and his gaze flickered toward Eli. "You know there's a chance he'll catch up with us before Wichita, right?"

"Then he'll find a hornet in his henhouse," Paul said. "Nobody chases one o' mine without answerin' for it."

Jody shifted. "You willin' to die for this, Paul?"

Paul stared at him. "Ain't about dyin'. It's about livin' with what comes after if we don't stand up now."

"I know I'm asking you all to risk your lives." Eli looked at each of them in turn, something unyielding in his eyes. "But I ain't got anywhere else to run."

The others nodded, and for the first time since they'd left Bailey under a pile of rocks, Paul felt a sense of shared purpose. They'd get Eli to Wichita and make sure he was safe, no matter what came next.

Paul's eyes wandered toward the horizon. *Come on, Rickett. We'll be waitin'.*

Chapter Fourteen

Jon shifted in the saddle, eyes narrowed on the horizon as the trail stretched before them.

Layton rode in silence beside him, a dark mark slashed across his cheek, still raw from Jon's punishment. The burn hadn't healed cleanly, and it shouldn't—failure came with consequences, and Layton's inability to capture Elsie when he'd caught up to her was as bad a failure as they came.

"Keep your head in this one, Layton," Jon said. "I won't be patching you up again if we slip."

"I've got it under control. Last time was a fluke."

"A fluke that left her riding free and me wasting more time. Don't test me."

"They was shootin' at me!"

"You forget why we're out here, Layton?" Jon asked.

"No, sir."

"Then start acting like it. This ain't some game."

"Wouldn't have thought you'd still be this worked up over her," Layton muttered.

Jon's hand twitched toward his holster, but he stopped short. "You're still alive because I need you. Don't make me rethink that."

Layton said nothing as they kept riding north.

Jon had originally sent Layton to buy some beef from a cattle drive near Fort Reno so they could keep looking for Elsie. Then, Layton *found* her—with that very cattle drive, of all things—riding among them, disguised as a man. Jon's lip twitched in amusement. *Clever, as always.* That sharp mind of hers had been both a thorn in his side and one of the things he admired about her the most.

"You sure she won't just run again?" Layton asked.

"She's got nowhere to run."

"Don't mean she won't try."

"What're you tryin' to say, Layton?"

"She has men watchin her, boss." Layton glanced toward the horizon. "Maybe it'd be easier to just let 'er—"

"You finish that sentence, and I'll burn ya properly this time." Jon spurred his horse ahead.

They crested a low rise, and there it was—a scattered group of cattle grazing near the banks of a narrow creek, a few riders patrolling the edges. Jon reined in his horse, squinting into the distance.

One of the riders caught his eye. How they moved in the saddle, the way they handled the horse—it could only be her. *Elsie.*

A slow smile spread across his face. She'd taken on the mannerisms of a man well enough, but Jon would know her anywhere. She could wear all the hats in the world, but she couldn't hide from him.

He nodded once.

Layton nodded curtly in return, though his eyes held none of the satisfaction Jon felt.

Jon scanned the distant cattle crew patiently, leather creaking under his grip as he flexed his fingers around the reins. A soft breeze tugged at his coat, carrying the scent of dust and cattle.

Layton shifted beside him, his hand resting on the butt of his pistol, though Jon hadn't given the order.

They had to wait for the right moment.

"Keep your eyes sharp. We make our move tonight."

Jon and Layton followed the crew until they made camp that evening. As the sun dipped toward the earth, they slipped from their horses and led them into the cover of a nearby rise, measuring every step.

Jon crouched and motioned for Layton to do the same.

Jon moved like a shadow, dirt barely crunching under his boots as he led the way. They kept low, pressing their bodies against the incline. Jon's hand drifted to his knife, testing its weight, and he felt a familiar surge, the thrumming pulse of adrenaline that emerged just before the hunt.

They wouldn't go for Elsie tonight. No, she'd scream and make a ruckus. *Why go through so much trouble when there's a much simpler way?*

Jon had spent years learning to hunt, back when he was barely old enough to hold a rifle. He'd started with game, but it wasn't long before he'd traded the woods for the road—and animals for men.

People thought they were harder to hunt, but Jon knew better. Men were predictable—fearful. When they thought no one was looking, when they thought they were safe, they made mistakes. That's when he struck.

He'd built a reputation on those mistakes.

Jon's eyes flicked from one figure to the next, mapping out their movements, the way they interacted.

Now... Which one of you is my prey?

He'd always had an instinct for reading people. The ones near the fire likely carried more authority. He knew by the subtle confidence in the way they held themselves that they'd be harder to break. The ones on the outskirts, now—drifting in and out of the light, always on the edges—they were the weak links.

It wasn't just about numbers. It was about leverage, knowing who'd fold under pressure. And if there was one thing Jon excelled at, it was making people bend.

You two.

Two men, one broad, one wiry, sat apart from the others, farther from the fire, their voices rising occasionally in drunken laughter. *Perfect.* Drunk and distracted.

It wouldn't take much to grab them.

Fear worked best when it came in the dead of night. Men were softer with darkness wrapped around them; they felt invincible until someone stepped out from the shadows and reminded them how wrong they'd been.

Jon had seen it countless times—the way a man's bravado melted away when he realized he wasn't alone, that every inch of distance from the safety of his group cut another thread of hope loose.

Tonight, he'd cut those threads himself, one by one.

Jon signaled with two fingers, and they moved in silently, stepping from shadow to shadow, cool as skunks in the moonlight. Crouching behind a cluster of rocks, Jon watched the broad one take a swig from his bottle, his words slurring as he leaned toward the wiry one.

Jon's breathing slowed as he tightened his grip on his knife, eyes fixed on the smaller man, who leaned back, laughter bubbling from his throat. Layton moved in on the broad one. *One step at a time.* They were close now. One wrong move, one slip of the foot, and everything could spiral out of control.

Jon counted the seconds, waiting for that perfect moment, when a man's guard dropped completely. Muscles coiled, he leaned forward, every fiber attuned to the prey in front of him.

One more breath, and it'd all be over.

As the broad one let out a loud bark of laughter, Jon motioned once, and he and Layton lunged.

Layton clamped his hand over the broad one's mouth and flashed his knife, pressing the blade against the man's throat. He thrashed, instinct kicking in, but Layton's grip tightened, cutting off any chance of a fight. It seemed Leyton's competence had finally returned.

Jon slammed the wiry one into the dirt before he could shout. A low groan escaped the man's lips as Jon knelt on his chest and pressed a hand to his mouth while holding a knife to his neck.

"Move, and I'll make sure you don't see another sunrise," Jon whispered.

The man froze, his eyes wide with panic. The other sobered quickly as Layton held him still, his knife gleaming in the moonlight. The struggle drained out of both men within moments, their bodies going limp under Jon and Layton's grips.

Jon leaned close to the wiry one's ear. "You're gonna be real quiet now. We don't want your friends hearin' about this just yet, do we?"

"I—I don't know what you want."

"You don't have to do this," the broad one muttered.

"Not a sound, or I'll cut you from ear to ear."

"Please, I'll—"

"Shut your mouth, before I shut it for you," Leyton hissed.

"Now, now, Layton, don't be so rude. These men are to be our guests."

"What...?"

Layton chuckled. "You really should think twice before wanderin' this far from camp."

"What do you want with us?"

"With you? Nothing. With the girl in your camp? A lot," Jon said.

"Girl? There's no girl in our camp."

"Just 'cause you're too dumb see somethin' don't mean it's not there."

"Please, we don't know nothin' about no girl! We're just driving cattle," the big one insisted.

"Don't matter if you know her or not." Jon's fingers dug into the thin man's shirt, dragging him closer. "You'll help us regardless."

"Please, just let us go—we won't blab, I swear. God's honest truth."

"God ain't here." Jon's eyes hardened. "Only me—and I ain't nearly as forgiving."

Without another word, Jon jerked the man up by his collar and dragged him toward the tree line. Layton followed suit, pulling the broad one along with him, his knife never leaving the man's neck. They moved like ghosts, disappearing into the darkness, their captives stumbling behind, helpless and silent.

We'll be together again soon, Elsie.

Chapter Fifteen

Near Caldwell

Paul thought Rocco and Jody had gone hunting, but Elsie wasn't so sure.

Yes, they'd been distant ever since that mess with Bailey, but they'd never wander off without notice before. The pair might've been rowdy, but they weren't stupid. Rocco was always talking big, pretending he'd seen it all, but he never missed an opportunity to boast about his sense of self-preservation.

He'd been a fixture of the camp, leaning his broad frame against a tree or towering over the fire as he recounted exaggerated tales of past exploits.

Jody, for all his rough edges, wasn't reckless either. He kept his head down, followed orders, and stuck close to Rocco.

Then, they just vanish, mere days after Layton showed up?

Too convenient.

As she brushed down her horse, Marcus approached. He glanced around camp, then jerked his head toward the trees, indicating he wanted a private word with her.

Well, with *Eli.*

Regardless, Elsie nodded and followed him.

Marcus had proved himself a man of few words since Elsie had met him back in Oklahoma. She'd heard rumors about where he came from, but for some reason, no one dared ask outright. He wasn't the kind to look for trouble, but he sure as hell knew how to end it when it came his way. The way he'd sent Layton scurrying to the hills proved that.

Marcus led her past the edge of camp, down where the undergrowth grew wild, then stopped. He pointed to a patch of disturbed earth.

Elsie looked down to see broken twigs, boot prints, and other signs of a struggle.

What happened here...?

Marcus knelt and brushed a finger over the churned earth. "These ain't no animal tracks."

"What are you sayin'?"

Marcus gestured to the overlapping prints. "Too many for just two men wanderin' off."

"You sure they weren't messing around? Rocco gets awful roostered sometimes."

"Rocco talks big, but he ain't dumb enough to wander far. Especially not with Jody followin' close behind."

"You think someone took 'em?"

The only ones who could've taken Rocco and Jody were Jon and his crew, and Elsie was reluctant to entertain the idea that Jon took them because of her.

"Somethin' happened out here, that's for damn sure." Marcus rose. "The way the dirt's stirred, weren't no accident. Someone dragged 'em off."

"Wouldn't we have heard them?"

"Maybe we weren't payin' enough attention."

Elsie's stomach tightened. "Paul's not gonna like this."

Marcus shrugged. "He'll like it less if we say nothin' and lose 'em for good."

"I…" Elsie's mind raced, but her voice faltered.

"Can't think who else woulda gone after Rocco and Jody instead of the cattle, but you know this gang better than I do. I'll leave it to you whether to tell Paul or not. I'm sure you'll make the right call." He stood and ambled back to the camp, leaving Elsie alone with her churning thoughts.

She'd stood there, chewing over whether to tell Paul or keep it to herself.

The scuffle might mean nothing. Might mean everything.

Keeping quiet might keep things calm, but calm didn't last long in her world. It never had. Running from Jon had taught her that some choices, no matter how safe they seemed, ended up trapping you worse. She couldn't shake the feeling that this was one of those moments. Ignoring the signs might mean losing Rocco and Jody for good.

They don't deserve that.

Her predicament gnawed at her all morning. Elsie kicked at the dirt, chewing on Marcus's words. He and Paul moved around her, but her eyes kept drifting to the edge of the trees. She bent to pick up a stray length of rope, twisting it between her fingers, anything to keep her hands busy, to keep the questions from clawing up her throat.

What do I do?

She puttered around camp until Paul decided they'd waited long enough and started preparations to leave. He seemed as calm as ever, checking his gear and muttering absently as he adjusted the rifle on his shoulder.

Her heart kicked up, words stumbling over each other in her head.

What if it's nothing? What if dragging Paul into it just makes things worse?

She wanted to stay quiet, to let him ride off without adding to his worries, but Layton *had* shown up, and now Rocco and Jody were gone. What if she said nothing, and the worst happened?

I've lived through enough silence.

Paul was about to mount his white mare when her tongue broke loose.

"I think Jon took Rocco and Jody," she blurted. "Marcus found signs of a fight."

Paul blinked, one hand resting on the saddle horn as his gaze scanned the camp. "Why d'you say that?"

"Hunting doesn't take this long, Paul."

"You sure?"

She stepped closer to him. "Yes."

Paul's fingers traced the leather strap of his rifle. He took a slow, deliberate breath as the wind kicked up, scattering dust between them, and squinted toward the horizon. The open plains always seemed vast, but now, Elsie felt like they were closing in, narrowing down to a single, looming question.

"Marcus doesn't jump at shadows." Paul nodded slowly. "We'll handle it when I come back."

"What?"

"No savin' anyone if we starve to death." He mounted in one fluid motion, the animal shifting under him. "Stay here. I'll be quick."

He glanced at her, his eyes lingering just long enough to suggest he wasn't entirely at ease leaving her behind, before nudging Dusty forward. A cloud of haze rose in his wake as he headed toward the tree line.

Damn it.

She'd have to wait.

Why would Jon want Rocco and Jody? Could he be intending to trade them for me?

Oh, that was something Jon would do. She could only hope that Paul would find a way to save them before it came to that.

***

In the hours that followed, Elsie busied herself with anything and everything to push back the thoughts pressing in. She focused on the cattle, checked the tack, and organized the supplies. Her hands kept moving, but her mind wouldn't stay quiet, drifting back to Jon, back to nights when his anger had flared like hellfire.

To the night she lost her best friend.

Fanny had supported her the first time she'd run from Jon, hiding Elsie in her hope chest so she could slip out of town after dark. The wood had smelled of lavender, a scent Fannie always wore. Elsie had squeezed her eyes shut, heart pounding so hard she could barely breathe.

But Jon had found her easily, his boots heavy on the floorboards. He hadn't spoken, hadn't yelled—simply raised his gun and pulled the trigger. Fannie's body had crumpled, her eyes wide even in death.

The longer Paul was gone, the more Fannie's death played on a loop in her mind, the echo of that gunshot as loud as if it had just gone off. Her skin felt too tight, too dirty. She needed to wash, to scrub off the past, if only for a moment.

When she got to the river, Marcus was already there. He stood a few feet from the riverbank, boots half-buried in the mud, eyes fixed on the rushing water.

"Water's runnin' fast today."

Elsie knelt and dipped her hands into the cool water. She watched the ripples spread around her fingers, thinking how easily the current could sweep away anything too fragile to stand firm against it.

"What's got ya by the river, Marcus?"

"Just watchin' the cattle, same as always."

Elsie splashed water across her arms, the cold biting into her skin. The river didn't care whether she felt dirty or not; it would keep moving, just like everything else. She shivered, though the sun still hung high.

"You gonna bathe?" Marcus tapped his fingers against his biceps. "It's mighty cold."

"I'll warm up later." The words left her mouth with an ease she didn't feel. She looked past him, out toward the horizon where the land and sky met in an endless stretch of nowhere. Jon was out there, somewhere, looking for her.

Marcus squatted on the bank, trailing his fingers through the stream as if testing its pull. He stood up frowning but sighed. "If you see trouble, don't try to be a hero."

She laughed, though the sound didn't carry. "Who said I was the hero type?"

"Well, just keep it in mind." Marcus brushed his hands against his pants and gave her a curt nod.

The wind picked up, tossing a few loose strands of Elsie's hair across her face as Marcus turned and walked toward the herd.

For a moment, she wondered whether he suspected her secret, but quickly dismissed the idea. The fact that he left her alone to bathe didn't mean he knew she was a woman. He probably always took care not to invade people's privacy.

She made her way toward a section of river flowing among thick brush and trees. The air stilled as she stripped down and slipped into the water. The world around her blurred, the sound of rushing water filling her ears. She closed her eyes and submerged herself fully, letting the cold bite into her bones.

Oh, I needed this.

Elsie moved deeper into the water, her hands brushing over her skin, trying to scrub away the memories that clung to her like mud. She dipped under again, letting the chill pierce through her bones, clearing her head. Rising, she took a breath, eyes on the vast expanse of uncaring sky. The weight of the trail fell away, and she was just a woman washed clean by the river.

Fannie's face flashed through her mind again.

The way her friend had smiled that last day, her voice soft as she helped Elsie pack her few things into the chest. The plan had seemed foolproof—leave under cover of night, escape Jon's grasp before he had a chance to find them. But Jon always found them. Fannie's blood had soaked the floorboards, her body crumpling as Jon dragged Elsie back. No matter how many times she scrubbed her skin, that memory never washed away.

Then, a rustle.

Her eyes snapped open, breath catching in her throat. She ducked, instinctively curling against the riverbank.

The rustle came again, louder this time, and her heart leapt into her throat. She crouched low in the water, her fingers wrapping around a stick beside her, her eyes darting toward the source of the noise. For a moment, the world narrowed to that patch of bushes, her mind racing through a thousand possibilities.

Another rustle, closer now.

Her grip tightened on the branch. A figure pushed through the undergrowth with slow, deliberate steps.

Then she recognized the large frame and careful movement.

Paul.

Elsie froze, half-submerged in the river, droplets of water clinging to her bare skin. Her curly hair, now fully wet, could not hide her delicate features. Her shoulders and slender arms were exposed, the lines of her body unmistakably feminine in the dappled light.

Her pulse quickened for a different reason. Her breath came short, and she grabbed the stick tighter, unsure whether to yell, to scream, to—what? She wasn't sure how he'd react.

Because he'd seen her.

He knows.

Chapter Sixteen

Near Caldwell

Paul stepped toward the riverbank, his eyes catching something—a splash, movement beyond the trees. His footsteps slowed as he neared the water's edge, and that's when he saw someone in the water.

Eli?

It looked like Eli, but... Paul fought to make sense of it. He stood frozen, watching as Eli tilted his head back, long wet hair plastered against his shoulders. The water glistening off his skin and sliding down his... *breasts?*

Eli was a woman.

Paul's eyebrows shot up as realization hit him. His lips parted slightly, caught off guard for the first time in a long while.

Eli's odd evasiveness, the strange way he—she—held herself at times, made sense now. Paul supposed he should have been shocked or betrayed, but all he felt was... clarity. She'd been hiding, running, and now, he knew why.

As he stepped out from the brush, her eyes locked onto him, and her face paling.

Before Paul could utter a word, a large stick hit him square in the chest with a dull thud.

He sighed, taking a deep breath as he looked down at the piece of wood now lying at his feet. He rubbed his chest, more out of exasperation than pain, then raised his hands slightly in a show of peace.

"Easy..." He took a cautious step toward her. "I ain't here to—"

The pounding of hooves interrupted his words. Both he and the woman turned toward the far side of the river. Through the trees, Paul could make out three riders, moving fast—and headed straight for them.

Paul pulled his gun from his holster. "Get down!"

Not-Eli's eyes widened, panic flashing across her face as she scrambled to the riverbank. "Paul—"

The first shot rang out.

Else ducked, and Paul stepped into the river, wading in waist deep as he took aim. Another shot cracked, and Paul returned fire. Water erupted in sprays as bullets struck the river's surface, and Paul could feel the current pulling at him, threatening his balance. He fired again, forcing one of the riders to swerve sharply. The same man Marcus had chased off—Layton, the woman who was Eli had called him—spurred his horse harder, cutting a path through the shallows.

Paul glanced over his shoulder at Elsie, half-submerged in the river.

"Keep your head down," he yelled, reloading with practiced efficiency. "This ain't the kind of trouble you want to meet head-on without—"

He'd almost said *without your britches*, but that wasn't the sort of thing you said to a woman—was it?

Another shot cut through the air, closer this time. Paul gritted his teeth and fired back, driving one of the riders back to the far bank. But they weren't giving up. One of them raised his rifle, aiming straight at Paul's chest.

A familiar voice cut through the chaos.

"Got your back!" Marcus shouted from the tree line.

Marcus's rifle boomed like thunder, and the man pointing at Paul pitched forward, tumbling from his horse and into the river with a splash, then disappearing into the current. The remaining pair of riders pulled back to the far bank.

As the dust settled, Paul finally saw them clearly.

"You've got something of mine," a dark eyed, tall man called, his eyes cutting to not-Eli. "Give her back."

She went still, her breath coming in ragged gasps.

"Come out, Elsie!" the man barked. "You ain't getting away this time."

So that's her real name—Elsie.

Paul took a step forward, his broad chest rising and falling slowly, like a man who had no need to rush. His eyes locked onto the man. "She ain't yours. She's with us."

"Is that so? You don't even know what you're dealin' with." His eyes flicked to Marcus, who stood motionless, rifle steady in his hands. "You hear that, old man? You're backin' the wrong horse."

"I hear plenty," Marcus replied, "but I ain't the one runnin' scared across a river."

"You want to get brave? Fine! But know this: we've got your men. Rocco and Jody, they said their names were. You want them back? We'll trade—her for them."

Paul's stomach dropped, but his face remained stoic. He glanced back at Elsie, who hadn't moved, her face frozen in shock and fear.

The man's gaze lingered on her. "You've always been mine, Elsie. Always will be."

"You ain't taking anyone," Paul said.

The man's smile widened, but his eyes remained cold. "I'll be back, and when I come, you'd best have her ready. Otherwise, I'll be sending your boys back one piece at a time."

With that, the man turned his horse, nodding to Layton, and they disappeared into the trees. Everything went quiet, the only sounds the distant rush of water and the echo of the man's threat in the air.

Paul stood there for a moment longer, eyes fixed on where the two had disappeared. Behind him, Marcus approached slowly. He didn't speak, but Paul sensed something in the way he moved, rifle still in hand.

The older man wasn't surprised. Not about Elsie, not about the men.

"You knew," Paul muttered, glancing over his shoulder.

Marcus shrugged, not denying it.

Paul looked down at Elsie, who still crouched, drenched, in the river. "Get dressed. This ain't done."

Paul turned around to give Elsie some privacy.

Once she was decent, she trudged up the riverbank, the hem of her shirt sticking to her thighs, hair plastered against her cheeks. Her eyes darted toward the far bank, but the hardness in her jaw never wavered. She was shaken, no doubt, but even now, barely covered, trembling from cold and adrenaline, she stood tall.

Girl's got grit, got to give her that.

"Get dry," Paul muttered.

As Marcus led Elsie to the campfire, Paul stalked toward the horses, his mind spinning with questions. The shootout, the man's words—none of it sat right. There was more to this than just some gang chasing after a runaway. The fact that Marcus had known Elsie's secret all along only made Paul's gut twist tighter.

The group set to packing the camp.

Paul moved mechanically as he loaded up, his thoughts elsewhere. *Rocco and Jody.* The image of them trapped, possibly tortured, gnawed at him—but it was the man's taunting voice, calling Elsie "*his,*" that really dug under his skin. It wasn't long before the questions he'd buried boiled over.

He marched up to Elsie, who sat wrapped in Marcus's spare coat.

"We need to talk."

Elsie's eyes flicked up, but she didn't say a word.

Paul crouched in front of her. "That man back there. I assume that's Jon Rickett. You mentioned he was after you before, and I didn't pry, but now—Now, the time for secrets is over."

"I told you before," she whispered. "He's after me 'cause I ran away."

"Why? What's so special about you that he'd chase you so far?"

Elsie's face paled, but her eyes glittered. "I never wanted to drag anyone else into this."

"Too late," Paul retorted. "If you want to keep Rocco and Jody alive, you better start talking."

Elsie looked down.

Paul began to think he was going to have to shake it out of her. He really didn't want to do that. Not only was it inappropriate to shake someone after they'd just been shot at, but Eli—Elsie—was his friend.

Even if she'd deceived him.

"We're married." Her whisper was so quiet Paul barely caught the words. "I didn't choose him. He took me from my father as 'payment' for an imagined insult and forced me to... I've been running ever since I escaped."

Paul blinked, trying to process her words. *"Married?"*

Elsie nodded, a bitter smile tugging at the corner of her mouth. "That's what he calls it. But I was never more than his possession. A trophy for him to look at and use whenever the need struck him."

There was one thing Paul just couldn't wrap his head around. He'd heard of Jon Rickett's gang before—small-time, but brutal. Elsie was kind. Capable. Clever. How had her spirit survived living with a man like Jon Rickett?

What kind of hell did you endure?

He thought of the times he'd caught her in quiet moments, the guarded way she spoke, the way she'd deflected his questions. Her silence had been a shield. It made sense now, the weight she carried, the way she never really let her guard down—not even once she'd found a place among them.

"Why didn't you just keep running?" Paul asked. "If you knew Jon wouldn't stop, why risk sticking around?"

"I didn't want to be found." She drew the coat tighter around herself. "I tried to get as far as I could, but... I needed money. Couldn't just keep running without food, without shelter."

"Pretending to be a man... you thought that'd be enough to keep him off your scent?"

"I never thought he'd look for me here. I thought it'd give me a chance to disappear, to hide until he gave up."

"Jon doesn't seem like the type to give up. You knew that."

Elsie nodded, her hands gripping the edges of the coat. "I did. But I had to try something. Anything. I... I couldn't live like that anymore."

Quiet stretched between them, and Paul saw a flicker of something in her eyes—a hint of vulnerability she rarely showed.

"And you'd have kept this up, wouldn't you?" Paul asked. "If he hadn't found you."

Her gaze dropped to the dirt, and she nodded. "As long as I could, if it meant staying free."

Paul stared at her. He should've seen it sooner. Should've noticed how carefully she'd protected herself, even when she began to trust them, even when she'd found her place in the group. He hadn't realized how deep her fear ran, how much she was willing to sacrifice just to be free.

"You're tougher than I gave you credit for," he murmured. "Most people would've broken by now."

"I've been broken before," she replied, "but that doesn't mean I'll stay that way."

"Why didn't you say somethin' sooner?"

She shrugged. "I've been running for so long, I don't know who to trust anymore."

It would've been easy to dismiss her, to leave her to Jon's gang and keep his own men safe. Rocco and Jody were already caught in this mess, and protecting her put them at risk. But he saw her strength, her desperation, and the courage it took for her to admit the truth.

Oh, who am I kidding? Giving her away was never an option.

"You're right," Paul said. "I don't like riskin' the men. But leaving you behind to face that"—he nodded toward the distant riverbank where Jon had disappeared—"ain't how I do things."

For the first time since she'd emerged from the river, Elsie's face lost some of its sharp edges. She wasn't out of danger, and they both knew it. Jon wasn't done, and the threat was far from over. But damn it all if Paul wasn't going to fight with everything he had.

"Marcus," Paul murmured, his eyes still on Elsie. "We're gonna get Rocco and Jody back. You in?"

Marcus's mouth quirked as he slung his rifle over his shoulder. "Wouldn't miss it."

"Alright. We pack up camp and figure this out. But know this, Elsie: you ain't running anymore. You're with us now, and we don't leave anyone behind."

Elsie raised her chin, her eyes gleaming. "I'm done running."

Paul nodded, his jaw set. "Good. Because Jon Rickett made a mistake comin' after one of mine."

Chapter Seventeen

Near Wellington

Elsie shifted in the saddle as the trio rode along in silence.

She kept imagining that this was all a bad dream. That Jon hadn't found her, that they'd find Rocco and Jody up ahead, hungover and stupid, but alive.

Marcus rode with the same calm intensity he always had, scanning the horizon like he expected trouble at any moment. Paul, though, was different today. Tense. His jaw worked under the thick stubble, his hands tight on the reins.

Rocco's hat was the first thing she spotted, a battered thing with a frayed brim, half-crushed underfoot. Her stomach twisted as her eyes darted down the trail. Jody's old leather pouch, the one he always kept tied to his belt, lay discarded further down.

Paul dismounted wordlessly and crouched near the belongings.

Elsie stayed put. If there was anything to find, Paul would find it. No need to look herself. No need to remind herself that Rocco and Jody were suffering Jon's "hospitality" because of her.

Paul grabbed the pouch, flipping it open, but whatever he saw made his face harden. The thing that fell out of the pouch looked like...

Please tell me it's not...

"We can't wait around no more." Paul stood up, holding a *tooth.*

Elsie saw the storm brewing behind his eyes, a sharp focus that unsettled her. His gaze swept toward the west.

"We head west," he said. "Off the trail. Toward the land ceded by the Seminoles."

"No!" The word left her mouth before she could stop it. "That's madness. You can't just—"

"You think stayin' on the trail's better? You think we got time to gamble on that?"

"You're not thinking straight!" Elsie gripped the reins harder as her heart pounded in her chest. "I don't want to gamble on you making the wrong decision. We stick to the trail, Paul, that's where our chances are!"

Her voice grated in her own ears, but the panic clawing at her was stronger. Every instinct screamed against heading into unfamiliar land. Paul had to see the danger, but his face was set like stone.

"We ain't got time to debate this." Paul's calm stoked her anger, like he wasn't hearing her, like he didn't *care*. "The trail is the first place they'll look, and we don't have the luxury of guessing wrong."

"You think heading west is some sure bet?" Elsie's voice pitched higher. "You're putting us all at risk—Rocco and Jody included. You don't know what's out there, Paul."

"And you do?" Paul's eyes locked on hers. "You'd rather walk into an ambush?"

"I've lived my whole damn life on the run! I know when something's a bad idea, and *this* is a bad idea."

Paul didn't budge. He loomed over her, waiting for her to finish. The wind whipped at his cropped hair, but he remained rooted to the spot, solid as the landscape.

Marcus shifted in the saddle, his gaze moving between the two of them before he finally spoke up. "Elsie, Paul's right. We can't risk staying on the trail. If they're trackin' us—and they are—they'll expect us to keep north. We head west, we've got a chance to shake 'em."

Elsie wanted to argue, but Marcus's calm delivery had pulled the wind from her sails. She stared at the ground, her anger folding into a simmering frustration that sat heavy in her chest. She hated that they were right. Hated that she didn't have another solution.

"Fine," she muttered, "but don't expect me to like it."

Paul's jaw unclenched. He mounted his horse and started west without another word. Marcus gave her a curt nod, then followed.

Elsie lingered a moment, staring down at the scattered belongings, feeling that familiar pull of dread settle into her bones. She'd agreed to head west, but the land beyond the trail was a vast unknown. There was no safety, no certainty. Only the promise of more running. More hiding.

How long must I hide?

She glanced at the sky, unable to shake the feeling that they were heading straight into the lion's den, but what choice did they have? Paul *was* right, loathe as she was to admit it. Jon's men were likely ahead of them, watching the trail.

With a heavy sigh, she mounted and followed the others.

The wind whipped through the open plains, thick with the scent of dust and cattle. Every so often, Elsie glanced at Paul, wondering how he could be so calm in the face of so much danger. She hated him for it, hated his damn unshakable nature, yet a part of her envied him. He always seemed to know what to do. Always sure. Always in control. She wished she had even a fraction of that steadiness.

She wished he'd been there to protect her when Jon first appeared.

The further west they went, the wilder the landscape grew wilder. The horizon stretched wide and empty, the land so vast it might swallow them whole.

Elsie watched Paul, who rode serenely, as if nothing could touch him. He'd made the call, and they were following blindly. Did he even know what he was leading them into?

Her horse shifted beneath her, and her heart leaped into her throat as movement caught her eye—a blur on the horizon. She squinted as three riders appeared in the distance, approaching swiftly across the open land.

Her body reacted before her mind had a chance to process. She turned her horse sharply, kicking its sides to push it into a full gallop, away from the riders, away from whatever danger they might bring. Her instincts screamed at her to run, to get as far from them as possible. Cold, unrelenting fear gripped her.

No. Don't just run away this time.

She went to Paul instead.

She'd always kept her distance, always tried to protect others by staying apart. But now, in this moment of blind panic, all she wanted was his protection. He was the only thing that felt solid, the only one she could run to.

Paul turned just as she reached him, his eyes narrowing in confusion before widening at the sight of the riders behind her. Without a word, he moved his horse between her and the approaching strangers, drawing his gun with the calm precision that defined him.

It's fine. Paul's here. He'll protect me.

Paul's gun was trained on the riders now, his body taut and ready to act. For a moment, the world seemed to still. Then, as the riders drew closer, something shifted in Paul's expression. His body relaxed, and he lowered his gun slightly.

"They're friends," Paul murmured. He kept his gun in hand, but tilted his chin in acknowledgment as the riders slowed to a stop a few paces away.

Elsie's breath hitched again as she took in the newcomers. They weren't members of Jon's gang. They were Natives— three men, their horses barely breaking a sweat from the hard ride. The man in front, tall and broad-shouldered with piercing dark eyes, nodded toward Paul.

"Hattak," Paul greeted him, a trace of relief flickering across his face.

"Paul Boone." The man nodded back. "It has been some time since we last met."

Elsie barely heard the words. Paul knew Natives? Not only that, he was friendly with them? How did one even get close enough to befriend them without being skewered full of arrows?

Hattak's gaze shifted toward Elsie. "You have new company."

"Yeah. Things have gotten a bit more complicated since we last crossed paths."

"How?" Hattak's face remained unreadable, but his eyes flickered; he knew more than he was letting on.

"We're being hunted. Jon Rickett and his men."

Hattak exchanged a look with the two riders beside him. "We saw them at first light. Two men with them—tied, not willing. They did not look well."

"You didn't speak?"

"It was not our fight," Hattak replied, "but now you are here. We will ride with you if you wish it. This land is harsh, and Big Jon brings trouble. Our knowledge will help, and together, we are stronger."

Paul fell silent.

Elsie watched him closely. Paul didn't like relying on others; she knew that much about him by now. Paul Boone preferred to keep his own counsel, to handle things on his terms.

But this was different. They *needed* help. And she wasn't sure if he'd take it. She wasn't sure if she *wanted* him to take it.

For a moment, she thought he might refuse. Then, he nodded. "We could use the help."

Elsie let out a breath she hadn't realized she was holding. Relief washed over her, tinged with curiosity. She'd seen hesitation in Paul's eyes, a moment of doubt. She wondered what drove his instinct for self-sufficiency. Was it fear of loss, or simply the need to remain in control?

Was it whatever had made him dread returning his ranch?

As they began to move again, Paul introduced the other two Natives as Tokabi and Sooni, members of the Choctaw tribe. After that, he rode ahead, and their new companions spread out to their flanks.

151

Elsie rode in silence, her thoughts churning. She watched Paul closely, trying to make sense of the man who'd become her protector. He was a mystery, one she yearned to solve.

Sooni, one of their Choctaw escorts, slowed her horse to match Elsie's pace. The woman gave her a small, reassuring smile, her eyes kind.

"You're safe with us," she said quietly.

Elsie nodded, though her mind still buzzed with uncertainty. She wanted to believe Sooni's words, wanted to trust that they'd made the right decision, but the danger was far from over. She could only guess at the path ahead; the only thing she knew for sure was that she couldn't outrun this forever.

But for now, at least, she wasn't alone.

Chapter Eighteen

Unknown territory, outside the Chisholm Trail

Paul rode beside Hattak, but his eyes weren't on the trail ahead. They lingered on Elsie and Sooni, off to the side of the herd, laughing like they didn't have a care in the world.

Elsie was showing Sooni how to lasso, a skill that came naturally. The rope flew, looping over the head of a wayward calf, and Sooni clapped, obviously impressed.

Seeing Elsie like this—free, even joyful—struck Paul in a way he hadn't expected. She'd been running, hiding, keeping to herself since he'd found out who she really was, and for good reason. But here she was, laughing as if all of that had been stripped away for a moment.

He watched her a little too long, his thoughts tangled. She was different now. Not just because she was a woman and not the man she'd pretended to be. No, Rickett had finally shown up and tipped his hand. It looked to Paul as if that had somehow set Elsie free.

It was hard not to admire her for it.

Hattak's voice broke the silence. "You've got a real knack for finding trouble, don't you?"

Paul blinked, pulling his attention back to the trail. "What're you gettin' at?"

Hattak tilted his head toward Elsie. "You're traveling with a woman now. Didn't see that coming. Especially not you, of all people."

Paul's jaw tightened. He wasn't used to explaining himself, so the words didn't come easily. He let the silence stretch, hoping that would be the end of it, but Hattak wasn't one to let things go.

"She's got you lookin' out for her, too," Hattak said. "Didn't think you had that in you."

Paul bristled. "Ain't what you think."

"Isn't it?" Hattak's brow lifted. "You usually ride alone. Seems like she's changed that."

"She didn't change anything," Paul grumbled. "I'm just helpin' her deal with some dangerous people, same as I would for anyone else."

Hattak's expression shifted, losing its teasing edge. "Big Jon Rickett—small-time but *nasty*. Don't turn your back on that one."

Paul nodded, scanning the horizon, more to give himself a moment than because he expected trouble. "We ran into some of his men not long ago. They've been trackin' us ever since. Rocco and Jody... he's got them now. I don't know what he plans to do, but I can't let it go."

"Hell of a mess you're caught up in." Hattak said. "You sure you want to go down this road? Men like Big Jon—they don't let up."

"I didn't ask for this, Hattak," Paul replied, "but I'm in it now, and Elsie—" He fell silent, unsure how to put his thoughts into words. "She's not just some helpless girl, runnin' scared. She's tough, smart, and stronger than she lets on. She's got her reasons, and I'm not lettin' Rickett take her back. Not when she's fought so hard to get away."

Hattak studied him for a moment. "You ever think you deserve more than just surviving, Paul? That, perhaps, you deserve to *live*?"

As accustomed to the midday sun as he was, Paul's skin felt hot. His grip on the reins tightened. The question caught him off guard, slipping under his defenses in a way he didn't like. Hattak better not have been insinuating what Paul thought he'd been insinuating. *She* had been the last. He'd never let himself trust like that again.

"Ain't got time to think about that. This life... it's what I know. The trail, the work, it's all I've got."

"Doesn't mean it's all you have to keep," Hattak said. "You fight for her. Maybe you should think about fightin' for yourself, too."

The idea sat heavy in Paul's chest, and he didn't much care to examine the way it made him feel. Fidgeting, he scratched at his overgrown beard to avoid the pity he imagined shone in Hattak's eyes. Paul had a job to do, and that job was keeping everyone alive, including Elsie. Dreaming about more than that—it wasn't in him. Not anymore.

"Survivin's enough for me," he muttered.

"Maybe. Just be careful. A man like Big Jon will take everything you care about, and he'll do it with a smile."

Hattak wasn't wrong; Paul knew that Rickett was dangerous, and going head-to-head with him wasn't something to do lightly. But Paul had made up his mind. Whatever Rickett had planned, whatever waited for them down the road, Paul wasn't turning back.

He'll never have Elsie again.

Paul hadn't expected to get caught up in Elsie's mess, but he couldn't imagine leaving her to fend for herself. He hadn't seen that side of himself in a long time—the protective side that wanted to make sure someone else had a future worth fighting for. But there it was, gnawing at him, reminding him that there was more than just staying alive.

A peal of laughter reached his ears, and he twisted around in the saddle to see Sooni, hands covering her mouth, a loop of rope dangling in front of her as Elsie shook with mirth.

Watching them, Paul found himself wondering what Elsie could be if she didn't have to run anymore. What kind of life she'd make for herself if Jon Rickett wasn't casting a shadow over it. He wasn't one to think about futures—not his own, and certainly not someone else's.

But Elsie was different. Something about her made him want to see her make it through this in one piece. Maybe it was just the trail, the way it wore down on people until all they had left was grit.

All he knew was that Elsie was nothing like his thrice-damned ex-fiancée, and he was satisfied with that.

When the time came to set camp, Paul dismounted with a heavy sigh. He rubbed his eyes and looked around. It was quiet—too quiet for the tension that had been eating at him since they'd found Rocco and Jody's scattered belongings.

Everyone moved with purpose, Marcus and Tokabi unpacking their gear while Hattak stood watch at the edge of the camp. Paul tried to focus on the task in front of him, hands working mechanically as rubbed the horses down, but Hattak's words kept pulling at the back of his mind. Paul kept thinking of Katherine—her smile, her laughter, the way she'd lit up the ranch. How she just... abandoned him.

Damn you, Hattak.

He glanced at the tent where Elsie and Sooni had disappeared earlier. The comparison between Elsie and his ex-fiancée wouldn't leave his mind. Elsie's laughter seemed more genuine, somehow. As if that woman had always been treacherous, and Paul just hadn't seen it.

Elsie and Sooni stepped out of the tent, but Elsie didn't look like a rough-and-tumble trail hand. She wore a simple dress—nothing fancy, but it stopped him in his tracks. Her hair, usually stuffed under a hat, flowed freely over her shoulders.

Paul wasn't sure what hit him harder—the way she looked or the fact that, for the first time, she seemed unsure of herself. She'd always been tough and independent, always so sure of her place—but now, standing in a dress that clearly made her feel exposed, she seemed almost... shy.

He caught himself staring and cleared his throat, stepping forward. "You clean up nice." It wasn't much of a compliment, but Paul wasn't one for flowery language.

She met his gaze, a flicker of surprise in her eyes, before her lips curved in a small, grateful smile.

Hattak, standing a few feet away, caught the exchange. Paul noticed the grin tugging at his old friend's mouth, the knowing look he shared with Tokabi before they excused themselves to patrol.

Paul shook his head, ignoring the amusement on their faces. Hattak could think what he wanted.

It didn't change anything.

The camp settled into a rhythm. They ate in silence for a while, each lost in their own thoughts. Paul sat near the fire, his mind still circling the decisions ahead, the path they were about to take. Then, Elsie sat down next to him.

He looked at her and kept looking. Up close, under the auburn light of the fire, she looked even more amazing.

She smiled, the delicate dip of her cupid's bow resting below the graceful line of her nose.

How could I have missed it? She's beautiful.

She nudged him with an elbow. "Must've been a while since you've seen a woman."

Paul blinked, caught off guard by her joke. Encounters with women on the trail were rare and, when they happened, he'd always treated them just like any other business transaction. He'd never traveled with a woman before, never came to care like he had with Elsie.

For a moment, he wasn't sure how to respond. Then, almost without thinking, the words tumbled out.

"Not since *her*."

The campfire crackled, and the world shrank down to just the two of them. Elsie's playful expression softened, and Paul realized he'd mentioned something he hadn't shared in years. He'd kept the past buried, locked away behind work and the trail.

"She was my fiancée," Paul continued, his voice steady, though the memories felt raw. "We had plans—a ranch, a future. She was everything to me, back before the war."

He paused, unsure why he was telling Elsie any of this. Maybe it was the way she looked at him, without judgment, just quiet understanding. Or maybe it was because, for the first time in a long while, Paul felt like letting someone in on the weight he carried.

"When I came home, she was gone, left to marry some merchant on the East Coast. Only a letter, saying how sorry she was." The words spilled out easily, the story that had haunted him for years finally slipping into the open. "After that, there wasn't much left to go back to. So, I hit the trail. Figured if I kept moving, it wouldn't catch up to me."

Elsie listened without interrupting. Something about her silence made it easier to keep going, like she understood.

Paul felt lighter, like he'd briefly set down a heavy load. Even knowing he'd have to pick it up again soon, at least for a moment, it wasn't his alone.

"Ain't told anyone that in a long time," he admitted.

"Guess we've both been running from things that won't stop chasing us," she said softly.

Paul looked at her then, really *looked*. She wasn't just a woman running from a man. She had her own ghosts, her own reasons for keeping everyone at arm's length. In that moment, Paul realized they weren't so different after all, both trying to survive in a world that didn't care if they made it or not.

The fire crackled between them, and for the first time in years, Paul felt like he wasn't alone.

Chapter Nineteen

Jon watched as Elsie's group approached slowly from the south.

His chest tightened, and his gut twisted. Damn Elsie for still being out of his reach, thinking she was free. Determination burned through him. He had to end this chase. The endless days and sleepless nights were wearing on him, but he knew he wouldn't rest until she was back under his control.

The late afternoon sun painted the sky a burning orange, clusters of sagebrush and the occasional lonely mesquite tree dotting the open lowland. The smell of horse sweat mixed with the dust in the air, a scent as familiar as the leather of Jon's saddle and the sharp tang of gunpowder.

"That them, Jon?" Kid pulled down the red bandana around his neck.

Jon raised his battered and stained hat. "That's them, alright." He didn't see Elsie, but there was no doubt in his mind that she was down there.

She has to be.

He glanced over at Layton, who rode silently on his other side, and nodded.

Layton spurred his horse and veered around the cattle drive, rushing to get to the buffalo heard to the north.

Jon had been waiting for days for Elsie's group to get here, specifically because of that buffalo herd. With their massive horns and shaggy coats, the beasts would provide the perfect distraction to allow Jon and his men to rush in, kill the trail boss and his assistants, grab Elsie, and get away with little hassle or loss of men.

Of course, the chaos would stop Jon from stealing the cattle, too, but it was a small loss.

Elsie's group got into position, and Jon signaled Layton.

Layton fired his rifle into the air. The exploding boom of the shot rang out, and the buffalo herd burst into motion, their massive bodies turning from calm beasts into a stampede of rolling power.

The ground quaked beneath Jon's feet. His heart pounded, and a thrill coursed through his chest as the chaotic mass of the buffalo herd surged toward Elsie's group.

"Damn... Can't say that's not effective..." Kid murmured, more to himself than to Jon.

The cattle of Elsie's group started panicking, and the trail hands rode around trying to contain it. Their shouts mixed with the bellows of the terrified cows and the rumble of buffalo hooves. The cattle crashed into each other, their hooves tearing up the dry earth and sending clumps of dirt flying.

One trail hand rode hard, his lariat swinging over his head before snapping out to catch a stray cow, pulling it away from the rushing herd. Another leaned low over his horse's neck, trying to steer the frightened animal through the chaos, dodging errant buffalo as they thundered past.

Jon smirked and gave the sign to attack.

His men rode in along the still-surging stampede. The trail hands, scattered and confused, didn't see them coming until it was too late. Gunshots cracked in the air. The trail hands all had old Spencer carbines, relics left over from the war, and they had to stow their lariats before they could use them. Jon's men had the newest Winchester models and the focus to fire.

Three trail hands fell immediately.

Jon spurred his horse forward, scanning every face, looking for Elsie's. His gaze cut through the dust and frenzied movements, his eyes wild, driven by rage and a longing he couldn't suppress. Every turn, every flash of an unfamiliar face brought a surge of desperation that twisted his gut tighter with each second.

As he rode, he pulled his Colt Single Action Army revolver from its holster and fired a few shots into the air to add to the confusion. Ahead of him, a man with a bushy beard jumped out from behind a wagon, brandishing his own pistol. Jon ducked, and the shot whizzed past his head. His heart pounded faster with the rush of battle.

He fired, and the bearded man crumpled to the ground.

A moment of satisfaction flickered in Jon's chest, primal and fleeting, swallowed almost immediately by the gnawing restlessness that ate at him like a festering wound, refusing to heal. He felt none of the relief he had hoped for; it was as if only Elsie's face, writhing in pain from the punishment he'd unleash on her, could quiet the roaring chaos in his mind.

The sharp tang of gunpowder stung Jon's nostrils. Trails of smoke drifted upward, partially obscuring the chaos, while the desperate cries of wounded and dying men reverberated through the haze. Nearby, a buffalo barreled into a wagon, splintering it into pieces, the force of the impact jolting through the ground.

Jon's men circled the cattle and wagons to the north, where most of the fighters were. Jon was about to follow when a rider emerged from among the cows, galloping south.

Short, with a small frame, the figure was covered by a duster that was obviously too big.

Jon pushed his horse south in pursuit. *It's her.* It *had* to be her. She'd run away from him, so it only made sense that she'd keep running now.

He closed in and grabbed her arm.

A wide-eyed young man turned to look at him, clean-shaven, but obviously male.

Jon growled and shot him.

"Damn it!" He wheeled his horse around and rushed back.

Layton, catching up on Jon's left, shot at a fat man in a black duster who'd been headed Jon's way with a rifle pointed at him. The fat man collapsed to the ground in a heap, and his horse bolted.

Jon nodded at Layton and moved toward a trail hand trying to hide behind a wagon. Layton veered left to relieve the group to the north, where the other trail hands had abandoned their cattle to focused on Jon's men.

Where is she? Why can't I find her?

The fight dragged on, giving Jon none of the pleasure he'd come to expect, no matter how many men he killed. The echoes of gunfire and dying cries of men and beasts melded into a numb backdrop, drowned by his racing thoughts. The moments stretched, each heartbeat throbbing with an urgency that eventually transformed into anger at himself—at his failure to find Elsie, to be just a step ahead for *once.*

Realizing that he was surrounded by the dead, alone with only the men he'd killed for company, Jon rode around the other side of the herd, but found no one else until he reached the northern side.

163

Layton was on foot, taking cover behind a water barrel as he exchanged shots with a pair of dark-haired trail hands, who had taken up positions behind a stack of hay bales. Kid Olson rolled on the ground as he wrestled a bald man. The rest of Jon's men were finishing off the remaining trail hands, who had barricaded themselves in the middle of three wagons, even as the buffalo continued to charge around them.

With Jon coming from the trail hands' backs, though, the fight would soon be over.

Jon fired in rapid succession, dropping the dark-haired trail hands. The bald man turned to look at Jon, giving Kid the opportunity to snap his neck. Kid looked up, blood dripping from his nose, and met Jon's eyes with a twisted grin.

Jon rode up to the men facing the barricaded resistance and looked at the men remaining among the wagons, searching for Elsie, but she wasn't there.

"Where the hell is she?" he snarled

He glared at Layton, who shrugged, his rifle still smoking.

Soon enough, the remaining defenders fell, the dust began to settle, and the echoes of gunfire faded into an eerie silence, broken only by the groans of Jon's wounded and the receding thunder of the stampede. The buffalo herd had disappeared into the distance, leaving behind a trail of destruction.

"I don't get it." Jon clenched his jaw. "How the hell isn't she here?"

"Because this ain't her group, Jon." Kid Olson walked up to him with a smirk. "You led us to the wrong herd."

Jon grabbed the front of Kid's shirt. "You think this is funny?"

Kid's smile faded, and his eyes narrowed. "What I *think* is that you keep messin' up. This is the fourth time she's slipped through your fingers. You should've never let her run in the first place!"

Kid's words struck a nerve Jon thought he'd long since buried, dredging up old resentments and feeding the slow-burning fire of discontent that had smoldered in his gut for years. When Kid's expression relaxed into something resembling contempt, a cold fury built inside Jon—wrath, sharpened by the sting of unspoken judgments and years of watching loyalty turn brittle around him. His jaw tightened, fists twitching with the urge to silence the Kid's insolence, once and for all.

Jon snapped.

He drove his fist into Kid's jaw, sending the man stumbling backward. Kid barely had time to regain his balance before Jon was on him again, fists swinging. Kid managed to land a blow of his own, catching Jon across the cheek, but he barely felt it. He drove his knee into Kid's stomach, sending him to the ground, wheezing.

Jon stood over him, panting, his fists still clenched, shaking with the adrenaline and anger coursing through him.

"Jon, enough." Layton stepped forward and put his hand on Jon's shoulder. "This isn't helping anyone. You need to think straight."

"Think straight? You think I need you to tell me what to do?" He pointed a shaking finger at Layton. "Don't think I don't know what this is about! You've always been soft on her. Always. I'm starting to think you care more about her than about me."

"Come on, Jon, we both know that's not true." Layton held his hands up, palms out. "I'm not betraying you—none of us are—but you're letting this obsession drive you mad. We need a *plan*, not a damned fistfight."

"Get out of my sight." Jon turned away. "All of you."

He clenched his teeth as the men moved away from him. As much as he hated to admit it, Leyton and Kid were right. Jon was the one who'd insisted on using the buffalo herd. The fact that they'd attacked the wrong caravan *was* Jon's fault.

He felt heat rise in his cheeks, and his eyes burned, his mind racing.

He still had the two hostages from Elsie's group; maybe that would be enough to draw her out. She had a soft heart, and she knew what Jon was capable of. She'd come running to save them.

He just had to make sure his men didn't betray him first.

Chapter Twenty

At the Ninnescah River

Paul urged Dusty forward as they approached the banks of the Ninnescah River. His shoulders relaxed at the sight of a large group of cattle and riders already there, especially when he spotted Margaret Borland—a legend among cattle drivers—standing proudly by the water. Her presence was a comfort; he'd heard of her success leading her herd through the swollen rivers last year when others had turned back.

Hattak, Tokabi, and Sooni nodded their quiet farewells to Paul and slipped away into the wild landscape. The plan had always been to part here. Paul's group needed to swerve north to get to Wichita and deal with Jon, while the three Choctaws would continue west toward the Council Grove, where Hattak would find himself a wife from the Creek tribe.

The fact that Margaret was here was happenstance, but Paul was glad for it.

Still, he regretted that the Choctaws had to go. Paul had always respected their quiet strength and connection to the land—something he himself had once shared with his father. Growing up on the northeastern border of Texas, Paul had learned to navigate the wilderness, read the land, track, and survive.

Those skills were the reason he'd survived the war, but the connection to and memories of his father they'd brought him had begun to fade after the battles ended and the memories of what he'd lost grew to eclipse them.

As his group approached the river, Paul squared his shoulders and rode to greet Margaret.

Margaret Borland, a fierce, self-possessed woman in a weathered hat and long coat, caught sight of Paul approaching. She raised her hand in acknowledgment, her eyes narrowing slightly under the brim of her hat.

Two young men with tanned skin and dark hair flanked her, both wearing denim trousers, button-up shirts, and hats that had seen plenty of wear, watching their herd for stragglers.

"Paul Boone." Margaret greeted him with a nod. "Pleasure to see you, sir."

"Howdy, Margaret." Paul removed his hat, a hint of a smile tugging at his lips. "I must say, you're a sight for sore eyes, ma'am. If anyone knows how to cross the Ninnescah without a fuss, it's you."

"Ain't no fuss about it, just patience and a little trust in the river." She chuckled. "Need help crossin'?"

"That, and somethin' else."

"Don't keep me in suspense, now. What is it?"

Paul glanced back and nodded at Elsie, who spurred her horse toward them. She was back in her shirt and trousers, her hair shoved under her hat. While her posture spoke of caution, the glint in her eyes was determined.

"The gal comin' our way is Elsie Wadsworth. She—"

"Oh, I know who she is." Margaret's eyes flicked over Elsie as she drew near. "Big Jon Rickett hollered louder than a bull in a branding pen the last time she ran away."

"What are you talking—"

A bark of laughter escaped the woman's wide mouth. "Can't hear the talk o' the town without leavin' the trail, Paul Boone."

He frowned.

"Don't you look at me like that. When was the last time you stepped into a town for more than a single night?"

Paul looked away. He didn't need to explain himself to anyone. His losses weren't things of the past; their ghosts walked beside him every day. The war, his ex-fiancée, his ranch—they all lived in the back of his mind, shadows that refused to fade.

Elsie brought her horse to a stop next to him.

"Elsie Wadsworth," Margaret drawled, looking her up and down. "The one who got away. For real this time, it seems."

Elsie nodded, lifting her chin. "Yes, ma'am."

"Well..." Margaret's lips pressed into a line that could have been disapproval or respect. It was hard to tell. "There's life beyond what's behind us, if we're willing to ride for it."

"I've been lookin' for it." A muscle twitched in Elsie's jaw. "Been running every chance I could get."

Margaret gestured for them to move closer to the riverbank, where the two young men and five extra trail hands were readying the cattle for the crossing.

"Running's not a bad start, but eventually you got to stand your ground. Come on—let's see if we can't get these herds across together." She turned her attention to Paul. "You plannin' to head back to Chisholm after this?"

"Right now, we're set on getting to Wichita. Spring rains have been hell, but we're making do."

Margaret nodded, her eyes on the river as the cattle began to make their way across under the guidance of the two young men and Marcus. She turned to Elsie. "How about you? Got any plans beyond runnin'?"

"I just want to be free of my past." Elsie's voice dropped to a whisper. "Free of Jon."

Jon Rickett weighed on her mind, and Paul knew it. She'd barely confided in him about what that brigand had done to her, but the haunted look in her eyes when she spoke of the past revealed more than words ever could. Jon had stolen her freedom, her family, and nearly her life. He'd forced her into a marriage that had broken her, and Paul had seen the scars— not just the physical ones, but those that she carried inside, holding her back from fully trusting anyone.

He wasn't sure just how much she trusted him, or whether it would hurt him if she didn't.

"I lost all three of my husbands, each one to this unforgiving life. Didn't know if I'd survive after the first. Thought I'd be better prepared after the second and the third." Margaret sighed, her eyes growing distant, as if remembering something from long ago. "Turns out, we never do get used to it. But there's life after marriage, Elsie. After loss. You can find happiness again. It's not the same, but it's there."

Elsie looked down. "I don't know."

"After my second husband died, I thought I'd never get back on my feet." Margaret looked at the cattle. The rhythmic movement of the herd mirrored the constant ebb and flow of the river it was crossing. "That was, until I realized that Alex and Jesse, my sons, needed me. Sometimes that's enough. You keep moving forward because it's all you can do."

"I don't have any sons, and I'm happy I don't." Elsie shook her head. "At least with Jon."

"It don't have to be sons." Margaret glanced at Elsie. "You just need to find something that makes life more than just surviving."

Paul looked across the Ninnescah, noting the way the riverbank twisted in the distance, lined with cottonwoods and willows. The river was treacherous, swollen from recent rains, and the banks were muddy, making every step dangerous for the cattle. Thankfully, the two young men—Margaret's sons, most likely—Marcus, and the other stable hands knew what they were doing.

The herd was crossing without problems.

Elsie blinked, her throat working as she swallowed hard and struggled to keep her emotions in check. "I'll go help Marcus."

Paul watched her ride away, his chest tightening with every inch she crossed. He hadn't realized just how much he wanted to keep her safe from anything—even memories.

Margaret smiled at him. "You care for her."

Paul stiffened. "She's a good hand."

It hadn't seemed so back when he'd met Elsie. She'd nearly drowned trying to cross the Washita, and despite her disguise, he'd sensed something was off. Her fierceness, her need to prove herself, reminded him of his younger self, back when he'd thought he had something to prove to the world, before the war had stripped him of illusions and left him with nothing.

"You can pretend it's just about the trail, Paul, but it's written all over your face." Margaret smiled, a knowing curve to her generous lips. "We both know it's true, whether you're ready to admit it or not."

Paul turned his gaze to the river, watching the cattle move steadily across, feeling a mix of emotions that left him uneasy. He'd never gotten close to anyone, not since the war. *Not since Katherine.* Returning from the war to find her gone, his ranch in ruins, had driven him to prefer solitude, the distance it gave him from others, the chance to avoid the pain of loss.

Now, though—now, things felt different, and that terrified him.

"Just make sure you don't let her slip away." Margaret clapped him on the shoulder. "People can be harder to navigate than the trail."

"Margaret..." Paul sighed. "Jon Rickett took two of our hands hostage. Will you help us get them back?"

She stared ahead at the cattle and her sons for a minute before she answered. "I'll help you fight him off if he comes for as long as we travel together. I won't seek him out, though. I'm sorry, Paul. I got too much to lose."

"No, I understand." He shook his head. "You have to look after your family. I respect that."

Margaret nodded and moved to help her sons, but her words stayed with Paul. He took a deep breath, his gaze following Elsie as she worked to guide the cattle. Perhaps Margaret was right.

Perhaps it wasn't just about the trail anymore.

Paul took a breath and spurred Dusty forward, heading toward Elsie, who was working to keep the stragglers in line. Her horse fidgeted at the water's edge.

Paul brought his own mount alongside hers and reached out to touch her horse's. "Easy, now."

She smiled at him.

"We're gonna have to push them a little harder." He nodded at the cattle hesitating at the river's edge. "Keep 'em moving."

Elsie nodded, her eyes flicking to the herd. She took a deep breath, her hands tightening on the reins. Urging her horse forward, she nudged one of the lead cattle with the toe of her boot, her voice rising to a sharp command. The animal bellowed a complaint, but it stepped into the water.

Paul moved beside her, his eyes scanning the herd for any signs of trouble.

The water was deep enough to reach the cattle's bellies, and their ears flicked back and forth nervously. One of the younger steers balked, trying to turn back, and Paul guided Dusty forward, cutting the animal off before it could break away. He waved his hat, his voice rising in a sharp shout, and the steer snorted, turning back toward the river.

Elsie was right there, her mount shoulder to shoulder with Dusty, her eyes scanning the herd just as his were. He found himself admiring the way she faced the challenge head-on, without flinching. Her curly hair rippled in the wind, and her heavy-lidded eyes often turned to him.

"Lookin' good." He told her, raising his voice over the din. "Just keep 'em moving, we're almost through."

"I got it." She smirked, her cupid's bow forming a perfect little V.

"Good to know you can listen to orders." He raised an eyebrow, doing his best to look stern, but the effect was ruined by the grin tugging at his lips.

173

"Only when they make sense." She scoffed playfully. "Don't get used to it."

Paul chuckled, shaking his head. "Just keep that herd moving."

The lead cattle reached the far bank, hooves scrabbling for purchase in the mud, and Paul felt a surge of relief. The Ninnescah was behind them.

He turned to Elsie. "Nice work."

"Thanks." Elsie smiled, and her eyes softened. "Couldn't have done it without you."

Something eased inside him at her words. He shrugged, but when he replied, even he could hear the affection coloring his voice. "Could've done more if you hadn't kept distractin' me from the cattle."

"Careful, Paul." Her eyes twinkled. "I don't know how long it's been since you spoke to a girl, but we consider that *sweet talk*."

"Oh, hush." He stared straight ahead as heat crept up his neck. "You know what I meant."

She chuckled and kept riding next to him.

Paul's heart pounded, and the warmth that had been comforting twisted into something unnerving. He swallowed, trying to gather himself, but Elsie's laughter still played in his mind.

What on earth has gotten into you, Boone?

Chapter Twenty-One

40 miles south of Wichita

The Ninnescah River glimmered behind them, a wide, slow snake of water splitting the rugged terrain at their backs. Margaret and her sons rode near the rear with their hired hands, the creak of leather and low calls to the cattle filling the dusty air.

Elsie rode beside Paul, her wind-tousled hair escaping from beneath her hat to catch the sunlight, which made it shimmer like spun gold. Her figure, lean but strong, moved fluidly in the saddle, her body shifting naturally with each step of her horse.

Margaret caught up to them, her horse moving easily alongside Paul's.

She nodded at Elsie. "You know your way 'round cattle."

Elsie smiled. "Thanks."

Margaret turned to Paul. "You're lucky to have 'er, you know?"

"I know."

Elsie tried to keep her eyes forward, but there was no mistaking the tension in her posture. She shifted in her saddle, her hands tightening on the reins, as if she was a breath away from bolting toward the horizon. She avoided Paul's eyes, but she couldn't hide the blush that crept up her neck.

It only made her more endearing.

They pushed on across an open stretch of plain, the sky wide and empty above them. Paul had a strange sense that things were *too* calm, the kind of stillness that pricked at his instincts. He let his eyes drift across the land, shifting with every roll of the hill, each ripple in the tall grass.

There it was—a shadow moving against the grain.

"Heads up!" He grabbed his pistol. "Riders!"

It came quickly, the way ambushes always did. One minute, the world was silent and wide open; the next, the air came alive with the thunder of hooves and sharp cracks of gunfire.

Paul and Marcus rode near the front, keeping an eye on the flanks. Margaret and her sons took the left side, the stable hands the right, while Elsie stayed closer to the rear.

Paul pulled Dusty sharply to the left, narrowly avoiding a bullet. He fired back, but his shot went wide. Margaret shouted orders to her sons and stable hands, directing their counterstrike. Dust and gunsmoke filled the air, stinging Paul's eyes as he kept his eyes open for Rickett. If he could kill the bastard now, Elsie would be safe.

It would all be over.

Paul scanned the chaos around him, his eyes darting from figure to figure as he fired at the outlaws. He caught sight of Elsie as she took aim at a rider bearing down on one of Margaret's hired hands. Her shot rang out and struck true. The rider crumpled in the saddle and fell to the ground in a heap.

Paul nudged Dusty onward, weaving between riders, then ducked low in his saddle, narrowly missing a bullet that whizzed by his head.

There!

Paul's eyes found Rickett as the bastard's horse pounded across the open field, moving erratically. Paul snapped the reins and gave chase, Dusty's powerful stride closing the gap inch by inch. Jon glanced over his shoulder, and seeing Paul on his heels, started shooting as he rode. Paul ducked, guiding Dusty with his knees as he returned fire, but Jon swerved to avoid the shot.

Everything narrowed to just the two of them; Paul's focus tunneled in on Jon alone.

Paul drew closer to Rickett, catching sight of the dust and foam on his horse's flanks, the tension in his shoulders. Paul raised his pistol again.

Rickett twisted in his saddle, the barell of his revolver flashing in the sun. The crack of the gunshot split the air, and Paul felt the shock vibrate through Dusty Rose as she let out a scream. Her legs buckled, collapsing beneath him, and Paul fell hard.

Pain exploded through his shoulder and side. Dust filled his mouth and nostrils as he rolled to a stop, aching from the impact. For a heartbeat, he lay still, struggling to push himself up among the vibrations of hooves pounding around him. His arms shook, but he couldn't afford to lie still. He planted his hands into the dirt, teeth gritted, forcing himself onto his knees. The world swayed, his vision blurring from the pain, but he forced his way through it.

He had to get to Rickett.

Paul drew himself up, his knees almost giving way beneath him. He raised his gun, his breath coming in ragged gasps. He fired. The shot went wide, kicking up dust near Rickett's horse, but not hitting him. The rattlesnake of a man looked around, then smirked and galloped away.

Margaret's voice cut through the haze, urging her sons and the others forward. Paul glanced up, his vision clearing just in time to see Margaret's sons riding hard, their rifles aimed at the retreating figures of the outlaws. The extra hands followed closely, guns blazing, keeping pressure on the fleeing gang members.

Elsie fired a shot that clipped one of the outlaws, sending him tumbling from his saddle. Marcus was right beside her, his revolver smoking as he picked off another outlaw who was struggling to regain control of his mount.

Soon enough, the gunfire died down, and the outlaws vanished beyond the horizon. Paul gritted his teeth. Jon Rickett had escaped, and the bitter taste of it stung as he struggled to his feet, eyes still searching, unwilling to accept that the bastard had slipped through his grasp.

On the ground beside him, Dusty Rose neighed with pain.

Paul turned and rushed to her fallen form. He dropped to his knees beside her, his hands moving over her neck, her mane as he swallowed the tightness in his throat.

A crushing grief settled over him as he realized what he had to do.

Dusty Rose had been his companion for countless miles— through storms, across rivers, over endless plains. She'd carried him tirelessly, her loyalty unwavering. Paul felt the familiar ache of loss twist inside him, a reminder of everything he'd already endured.

He knew there was no other choice. Letting her suffer wasn't an option, but the decision tore at something deep within him, another piece of himself chipped away by the harshness of this trail.

He reached for his gun, his hand steady, even if the rest of him was anything but.

Paul hesitated, eyes burning as his thumb brushing the cold metal of the trigger. He looked into Dusty Rose's eyes, her pain clear, and a flood of memories surged up—nights spent under the stars, her steady breath a comfort beside him, her strength carrying him through dangers and hardships.

His chest tightened, and for a moment, what he was about to do was unbearable. The trail demanded sacrifices, but this one cut deep, deeper than most. He swallowed hard, fighting against the urge to wait, to hope for another way.

There was none. Not here. Not now.

Paul pressed the barrel to Dusty's head, and his voice broke as he spoke. "Thank you, my friend... Thank you for everything. I'll never forget what we've been through."

He closed his eyes and, as a tear broke free to slide down his cheek, he pulled the trigger.

The sound boomed louder than any cannon he'd heard back in the war.

He buried his face in Dusty Rose's mane and exhaled slowly, then felt a gentle pressure on his shoulder. Scrubbing a hand over his face, he looked up to find Elsie, her hand resting lightly on his shoulder. Her warmth and the pressure of her fingers anchored him to the present, stopping him from descending into memories of the many losses he'd endured.

Squeezing his eyes shut, he stroked Dusty's white muzzle one last time. *Goodbye, my friend.*

He opened his eyes to the sound of hooves. Margaret rode up, her rifle resting across her lap, her eyes flicking to Dusty

Rose, then to Paul. She gave a short nod. Behind her, her sons kept watch, their eyes scanning the horizon for any sign of the gang returning.

"We'll make camp soon," she murmured. "Get everyone settled."

Paul stood, brushing the dust from his knees. He gave Elsie a look, and she nodded, her hand slipping from his shoulder. As he moved away, Margaret called orders to her crew, telling them to set up a perimeter and tend to the wounded. Paul's eyes drifted over the men, noting the weary but relieved expressions. They had made it through the fight, but there were still miles of trail and danger ahead.

He helped set up the camp.

As night fell, and everyone sat down to eat, Paul kept glancing at empty spots around the fire. Places where Rocco and Jody would've sat. Their absence was a hole in his chest, one that smelled of failure. He hadn't protected them. He'd known Jon Rickett was coming, yet he'd let them get captured. Marcus and Elsie did their best to mask the strain, but Paul knew better; their smiles were thin, their laughter forced.

It would be fine. It had to. He had to believe that.

He had to believe that they'd rescue Rocco and Jody, just as they'd free Elsie of Jon. Yet, he couldn't bring himself to say it. Those words would ease the tension in Elsie's shoulders and the fear behind her eyes, but he couldn't speak them.

He couldn't promise her that Rocco and Jody would come back alive when Jon could've already done away with them. He couldn't promise to free her of him when the bastard kept running and hiding, avoiding a straight fight by coming out in ambush after ambush until Elsie went mad.

She looked at him, her eyes meeting his briefly, and he gave a small nod. An unspoken understanding was forming between them, a bond forged through the fire of what they had faced. Paul knew she had his back, just as he had hers, and in a world as unforgiving as the trail, that meant everything.

And so, he would try. Whatever came to pass, he'd do his best to strike down the cockroach that was Jon Rickett.

***

They moved on with first light. The morning passed uneventfully, though it was difficult for any of them to relax, given what they'd been through the night before.

It was late afternoon when they came across the first signs of the Native camp—smoke rising in the distance, the faint drumbeats carried on the wind. Paul was surprised at the relief that settled over him, the tension in his shoulders easing. It wasn't just safety; it was the feeling of being close to people who knew this land, people who wouldn't be cowed by the likes of Jon and his gang.

"Didn't think you'd be happy." Elsie looked over, her brow furrowed. "They'll want ten cents a head to pass."

"Worth it for the respite from Jon's quick raids. I'm hoping to find some help there, too."

"That's a good idea." Elsie looked thoughtful, her eyes narrowing as she scanned the horizon behind them. "Jon fears the Natives. Don't have much experience with them."

"Then we use that."

"You think he killed Rocco and Jody?"

Paul's jaw clenched as he looked away, scanning the horizon. "If he did, he'll answer for it."

They parted with Margaret and her crew at that point, before they entered Indian territory proper.

"Take care." Margaret's eyes softened when she looked at Elsie. "Both of you."

Elsie hugged her, murmuring her thanks.

Margaret's sons were already guiding their horses, preparing to lead the small herd along a different path. They'd take a longer route, skirt around the Indian territory rather than pay to pass through it directly. It was a practical decision, one Paul understood, though it meant parting sooner than he would have liked.

Still, Paul said his goodbyes and watched them go.

Hopefully, his plan to find help in the Indian camp would bear fruit.

Chapter Twenty-Two

30 miles south of Wichita

Elsie had never set foot in a Cherokee camp before. The air was rich with smells she couldn't quite place—smoke from cooking fires mingled with herbs, an aromatic mixture that reminded her of the wilderness more than any camp she'd ever known.

She kept her eyes on Paul, her hand brushing against her horse's saddlebag as they walked into the camp. Everyone turned to stare at them, but Paul seemed comfortable, his body relaxed as he nodded greetings to those they passed.

He wasn't in any rush, his steps sure as they moved deeper into the camp.

Elsie had never encountered people like the Cherokee before. There was something different about the way they moved, a confidence that was almost unsettling. She didn't understand the significance of their gestures, of course, or the rhythmic language that flowed around her. In fact, everything about them felt odd—their closeness, the way they barely seemed to need words to communicate.

It was a kind of unity she'd never experienced, and it made her uneasy.

Paul approached a small group of Cherokee men, who glanced up, their eyes settling on Elsie for a moment before shifting to Paul. Just as Paul began to speak, Marcus appeared beside them, his face flushed.

"Didn't think you'd start without me." Marcus grinned and nodded at the Cherokee men. His eyes flicked over to Elsie.

"Got stopped by one of the kids—wanted to show me his rabbit."

Paul smiled, shaking his head. "You and animals."

"Can't help it. Animals just like me." He then turned to the Cherokee men. "I'm Marcus. We're grateful to be here."

The Cherokee nodded back, some smiling, and spoke with Paul and Marcus in that lilting language Elsie didn't understand. Marcus listened intently, glancing at Paul occasionally as they conversed.

After a while, Marcus leaned over to Elsie. "They're asking about the cattle—want to know if any are for sale."

Elsie nodded.

One of the men looked at Elsie, then back at Paul, saying something with a nod in her direction.

Paul smiled, nodding. He turned to Elsie. "He asked if you were my partner. I told him yes, and that you can handle yourself."

Marcus chuckled. "Should I be offended?" His grin took on a wicked edge. "Or is that not the kind of partner he was asking about?"

Elsie mock glared at Marcus and turned back to Paul. "Anything else?"

"He said you must be strong to ride alongside me."

Elsie let out a small laugh, shaking her head. "I think he's giving you too much credit."

The men spoke for a bit longer before the one of the Cherokee gestured for Paul and Elsie to follow. Elsie raised a brow at Marcus when he made no move to join them, but he just waved her forward, smiling, then knelt as two children approached him.

"Say, Paul." Elsie scratched her chin. "How come Marcus stayed behind?"

"I can only take one partner to see the Chief, and I didn't want to leave you alone. Not even here."

She understood his concern. Jon had already proven slippery, appearing out of nowhere more than once. The chances of him popping out from behind a bush to snatch her were low, but not zero.

Still, even with Paul next to her, she couldn't help the nervous flutter in her stomach. She wasn't afraid, but she was keenly aware of her outfit—worn wool shirt, leather chaps, hat pulled low over her eyes. She was dressed like a man, while every other woman here wore distinctly feminine clothes.

She tugged at the hem of her shirt and glanced at Paul.

He leaned in. "They're taking us to meet the Chief. Don't worry—all is well. He's expecting us."

He'd misunderstood, but she didn't want to correct him right now. Plenty enough time after they spoke to the Chief and their Cherokee minder left them alone.

They weaved between teepees, passing groups of children playing with sticks and running through the tall grass. Paul walked with an easy confidence she admired. It wasn't an act—he looked at home here, like he knew this camp as well as any other place. It calmed her own anxiety, though a flicker of worry remained.

She'd have to meet the Chief, present herself as Paul's partner. From the moment Jon had taken her from her father's farm, no man had treated her as an equal.

Would she be able to handle it?

Once they reached the Chief's tent, Paul exchanged a few more words with their escort before they went inside and sat with the Chief.

The Chief sat on a woven blanket, his demeanor calm and steady. Paul greeted him with respect, bowing his head as he spoke. Inside, the tent was warm, thick with the scent of burning herbs that filled Elsie's lungs, soothing her nerves, even as her heart pounded with anticipation.

Elsie let Paul do the talking—not that she had a choice, since she didn't speak the language—his hand resting on his knee as he described their journey and the herd they were driving. He spoke confidently, his voice steady, and Elsie again admired the ease with which he handled himself.

Paul gestured to her as he spoke, probably introducing her as his partner.

Elsie's breath caught for a moment as she met the Chief's eyes. His gaze was penetrating, but not unkind. He nodded, his expression softening, and offered her a brief smile of acknowledgment.

She returned it.

The Chief spoke, and Paul translated. "He welcomes us and respects the journey we have made. He says the bond between partners is what makes the trail worth traveling."

Elsie swallowed, feeling her face grow warm. "Tell him we're grateful for his hospitality and that we hope to honor his trust."

Paul turned back to the Chief and translated.

The Chief's lips curved into a faint smile, and he nodded to her again before turning back to Paul. After a bit more conversation, Paul unsnapped a small leather pouch hanging from his belt and held it out to the Chief, who accepted it with a solemn nod.

Paul turned to her. "I bought us two days of rest, safe passage, and..." He took a deep breath. "And a horse for me."

She nodded, noting the glint of moisture in his eyes without comment. Dusty Rose's loss remained fresh, and her heart ached for his loss. "Plenty enough."

"He also says we're welcome to share their food and sit by their fires as long as we show respect."

She frowned. "Isn't that what you paid for?"

"Not at all—that money's for passage, tepees, and leave to make our own fires on their land. He's honoring us because of our past dealings."

She smiled and inclined her head to the Chief. "Thank him from me as well, then."

Paul conveyed her message, and the Chief smiled back.

Then, the Chief gestured to an attendant, who left the tent quietly and returned carrying a small tray laden with food— savory stew thick with herbs, flatbread, and a pot of tea. He motioned for them to eat, and Elsie felt a wave of relief wash over her.

The agreement was made. They had two days to rest and regroup.

Elsie stretched they stepped back into the sunlight, then shrank in on herself as a pair of women walked past, the beads on the fringes of their dress clicking quietly as they went. Watching them, Elsie's earlier worry about her attire slammed back into her. Since she and Paul were waiting for someone to show them to their tepees, now was as good a time as any to bring it up.

"Paul... You think they'll be alright with me?" She looked around. "With... what I'm wearing?"

Paul nodded, a smile tugging at the corner of his mouth. "They know the strength of women. Ain't got anything to worry about."

"Good to know."

Paul looked up as a stocky Cherokee woman came to lead them to where they'd sleep. "Come on, Elsie, let's get settled."

Marcus had already been shown to his teepee; apparently, the Chief had harbored no doubts that Paul would pay. When they arrived, however, their lodgings turned out to be a single tepee.

"Paul..." Elsie frowned. "Why is she offering us a single tepee?"

Paul cleared his throat. Elsie could've sworn he was blushing, though it was hard to tell under that bushy beard of his. "I should've expected this."

"What?"

Paul rubbed the back of his neck. "They think we're—well, that we're a... couple."

She blinked. "What?"

"I don't think they understand the concept of a man and woman being partners and *not* a couple."

She raised an eyebrow. "So tell them we need two."

"Wait..." He scratched his beard. "Maybe it'd be safer this way. I've started expecting Jon to jump out of nowhere."

Elsie gave him a long look, then expelled a noisy breath. "Alright—but you keep to your side!"

Paul raised his hands in mock surrender. "I'll be respectful, I swear."

She believed him.

***

That night, the sounds of the camp around them slowly faded into the background, the fire casting soft shadows along the canvas walls of the teepee.

As Elsie watched the flames flicker, her mind drifted back to her father's farm. The nights there had been quieter, filled with chirping crickets and the rustle of wind in the trees. Here, the occasional laughter from outside, the rhythmic beating of a distant drum, and the soft murmur of far-off conversation created a different kind of lullaby. She felt a pang of homesickness, but also a strange comfort in knowing she wasn't alone.

"Paul... You'll stay alert?" Elsie asked.

"Always." Paul shifted in his bedroll to met her gaze. "Get some rest."

Nodding, Elsie pulled the blanket tighter around her shoulders. She closed her eyes, the sound of his breathing transforming the unfamiliar surroundings into something almost comforting.

***

The next morning, Paul and Elsie made their way to where the Cherokee kept their horses, a pen filled with restless movement, hooves stomping the earth, heads tossing. Elsie watched Paul examine the animals carefully, assessing each horse's size, the muscles along their legs, their teeth. However, there was a stiffness to his movements, a lack of ease that betrayed the fact that he wasn't entirely comfortable.

She stepped up beside him and touched his arm. "You want a horse that fits you, but also *trusts* you."

He pressed his lips into a thin line. "I need one that'll do the work. That's all."

Elsie shook her head. "It's more than that. Let them come to you. Let them see you first."

She moved closer to the pen, holding her hand out, palm up. A chestnut mare stepped forward, ears flicking as she sniffed Elsie's fingers.

Paul raised his eyebrows. "You make it look easy."

"It ain't hard. You just have to be patient." She stepped back. "You gotta let them choose you, too. Trust goes both ways."

Paul nodded slowly, his gaze shifting back to the pen. Moving forward, he mimicked her actions—hand out, movements slow and deliberate. The horses watched him, and after a moment, a dark bay stepped closer, nostrils flaring as it took in his scent. Paul froze, letting the horse come to him.

"That's it." Elsie's eyes stayed on him. "Nice and slow. Don't rush it."

Paul moved cautiously, his hand brushing the bay's neck. He glanced back at Elsie, the hint of a smile on his lips. "Guess you're right."

Elsie grinned. "I usually am. Walk around the pen. See if it follows."

Paul did as she said, his steps steady, his eyes on the horse. The bay hesitated, then moved after him, its head lowering slightly as it walked.

Paul glanced at her. "Guess you know a thing or two about this."

Elsie shrugged, her smile widening. "I've been around animals long enough, and they're not so different from people. You gotta earn their trust before they'll follow you."

He nodded and reached out to brush his fingers through the bay's mane. "Thanks."

"We're in this together." Elsie stepped closer. "Just like you said."

"Yeah."

"Now let's get you a saddle and see if you can stay on." Elsie winked at him.

Chapter Twenty-Three

30 miles south of Wichita

The morning after Paul had bought his new bay gelding, Spirit, he found himself in the wilderness yet again. Marcus followed just behind him, though Elsie had stayed behind. Paul wasn't concerned; Big Jon Rickett wouldn't dare go looking for her at the Cherokee camp, not if he was afraid of Natives.

Wohali, a young Cherokee with black hair tied into a braid and a wiry frame earned from a life outdoors, rode beside Marcus. He'd joined them as an extra hand; with Rocco and Jody gone, Paul was glad for the help.

Wohali hadn't been the fastest or the strongest of all the Cherokee that had volunteered, but Paul had known from the moment he saw the youth that it had to be him. He had a quiet intensity about him, a sense of calm focus that made him seem older than his years. He moved with natural grace, and each gesture he made deliberate.

The trio had brought half the cattle with them, trying to lure Jon's gang out. It was a risk, but a necessary one. Paul *needed* to end this, if he could, before Elsie left the Cherokee. It would mean a confrontation, of course, but Paul was more than ready.

Marcus guided his horse alongside Paul's. "You think he'll take the bait?" His usual grin was gone, replaced by a furrowed brow and an edge of tension that mirrored Paul's own.

Paul nodded, keeping his eyes forward. "He will. 'Big Jon' ain't one to pass a chance like this."

"Long as you're sure. We got half the cattle with us."

"He wants Elsie back mighty bad," Paul reminded Marcus. "Don't you worry about the cattle, neither. We've got another edge he won't see comin'."

"And that is...?"

"Made a deal with the Cherokee. They'll help us out. Gotta wait for the right moment, though. No sense tippin' our hand too early."

"Paul." Wohali joined them, speaking in his native tongue. "This man, Big Jon—he's dangerous?"

"More than dangerous." Paul met the youth's eyes, answering in the same language. "He's obsessed."

For a while, they went along with only the clattering of hooves and the occasional low or grunt from the herd. Paul kept his senses sharp, and it wasn't long before he spotted a flicker of movement along the tree line in the distance. He signaled Marcus and Wohali to slow down, his hand dropping to the rifle strapped to his saddle.

"There," Paul said, nodding toward the trees. "They're here."

Marcus squinted, following Paul's gaze. "You see him?"

Paul shook his head. "Can't make out faces yet, but he's there. I can feel it."

As they neared the edge of the trees, the outlaws rode out to meet them. Jon Rickett was front and center, his face twisted with hatred and possession. His men fanned out behind him, and at the very back of the group, Paul saw Rocco and Jody. The two looked battered, but they were alive, and that was what mattered.

Paul smiled. *The dumb bastard really brought them out.*

It was a gamble on Paul's part.

He'd planned to gun Big Jon Rickett down here if he got the chance, no matter what, even if he'd had to do it knowing he hadn't saved Rocco and Jody. Paul knew that, if their leader fell, none of the outlaws would have any reason to keep his men alive; however, based on what Elsie had told him about Jon, Paul had been willing to gamble that the bastard would bring his hostages out, just to taunt him—and he'd been right.

Big Jon stopped about a hundred yards away from Paul. "Give her up, trail boss. You can't keep her from me forever."

"Elsie isn't just a thing to be given, nor owned." Paul clenched his jaw. "You need to let this go."

Jon laughed humorlessly. "Let it go? You think I'm just gonna walk away? I'll get her back, one way or another. You must know that."

Paul's eyes hardened. "Then I guess we do this the hard way." He drew his rifle in one smooth motion and fired.

The shot rang out, and Jon's hat flew off as he ducked, spurring his horse to the side. Chaos erupted. Marcus drew his revolver, and quick as lightning, Wohali had his bow out, arrows flying toward Jon's men. Paul fired again and struck one of Jon's men square in the chest.

A sharp whistle cut through the madness.

A group of Cherokee warriors emerged behind Jon's men, taking the men holding Rocco and Jody completely by surprise. In seconds, arrows found their marks, and the outlaws holding Rocco and Jody fell from their saddles. The warriors moved in, cut the ropes that bound the hostages, and pulled them free. Then, without hesitation, the warriors turned and disappeared into the trees with Rocco and Jody clinging to them.

Paul kept shooting at Jon's men with a lighter heart.

The gunfire was relentless.

Paul fired again and again, dodging left and right, the recoil kicking back hard against his shoulder. Jon's men were scattered now, but they weren't retreating. Bullets whizzed past, snapping branches, kicking up dust, and panicking the cattle.

"Keep pushing 'em back!" Paul shouted to Marcus.

Marcus reloaded quickly. "We got 'em, Paul. Just gotta hold."

A shot rang out, close—too close—and something grazed Paul's arm. He gritted his teeth and ignored the pain. His eyes locked on Jon, who'd pulled back, trying to rally his men. Paul aimed his rifle, but Jon was fast, ducking low and spurring his horse behind a cluster of trees.

The heat of battle—the pounding of hooves, the crack of firearms, the shouts of men—raged all around Paul. His own heartbeat was a steady drum in his ears, his focus narrowing on every movement around him. His trio's superior riding skills allowed them to hold their own, even without cover, but Jon was still out there, and that meant the danger wasn't over.

Jon reappeared, spurring his horse straight at Paul, his revolver aimed right at him. Paul barely had time to react, jerking his rifle up and firing. The shot went wide, grazing Jon's horse, which reared up, throwing him off balance. The bastard hit the ground hard, rolling to avoid another shot as Paul took aim again.

I'm going to get him this ti—

"Paul Boone!" A translator from the Cherokee camp grabbed Paul's shoulder and turned him around. "They've got your woman!"

The words hit Paul like a physical blow. His stomach dropped, and for a split second, everything else faded—the gunfire, the chaos, the fight.

"Marcus! Wohali! Cover me!" He turned Spirit without a second thought, spurring him hard back toward the camp.

His world narrowed to the pounding of hooves and the rush of wind in his ears. Helplessness tore at him, and he wanted to claw at his chest. He had to reach her in time. Nothing mattered except getting to Elsie.

When they reached the outskirts of the camp, Paul spotted a cluster of people gathered, faces drawn in concern. He pushed through, his eyes searching until they landed on Elsie.

She was on the ground, dirty and scraped up, eyes wide with fear.

Paul approached and dismounted, and the Cherokee parted to let him through. He knelt beside her and reached out. "Elsie..."

She flinched away from him, her eyes unfocused, her breathing ragged. A sharp pang of hurt shot through him, her rejection stinging deeper than it should have, but he understood—this wasn't about him. This was about the terror she had just endured.

He pulled his hand back slowly, his voice softening. "It's me, Elsie. I'm here. You're safe now."

She looked at him then, her eyes filling with tears. "Kid...
Kid Olson came after me. One of Jon's—the worst. Mean and
violent." Her words tumbled out, disjointed and choppy. "Said
he'd be waitin' in Wichita, with or without Jon. Said it didn't
matter who stood in his way. Not Jon. Not you."

Paul's chest tightened. He clenched his jaw, fighting to
keep his expression calm for her sake. He reached out, his
hand hovering near her arm, careful not to startle her again.

"He won't touch you again." He put weight into each word
to show it was an ironclad promise. "I swear to you, Elsie.
Whatever it takes, I'll make sure of it."

She nodded, trembling as the tears spilled over, her gaze
dropping to the ground. Paul watched her, feeling a helpless
ache. He hated seeing her like this—scared, hurt, stripped of
the strength he knew she had.

"Rocco and Jody?"

Paul smiled. "They're fine. Beat up, but fine. The Cherokee
rescued them in the skirmish."

Elsie let out a shaky breath, and her shoulders slumped.
She wiped her face with the back of her hand. "Thank God."
She closed her eyes for a moment, as if she were trying to
gather herself.

Paul shifted, lowering himself to sit beside her on the
ground, close enough for her to feel his presence, but careful
not to crowd her. He wanted her to know that he was there,
that he wasn't going anywhere.

"We're gonna get through this," he murmured. "You, me,
Marcus, Rocco, Jody—all of us. Jon's not gonna win. Not
now, not ever."

For a long moment, she just stared at him, and the fear on her face slowly began to ebb and give way to something else— something like hope. It was fragile, but it was there. She nodded, a small, almost imperceptible movement, and warmth spread through Paul's chest.

She still believed in him, trusted him.

He stayed there beside her, waiting for the last of her trembling to subside. When it did, he reached out again, brushing his fingers against her arm. This time, she relaxed under his touch.

He'd been careless, and he knew it. He hadn't expected Jon to separate his forces, hadn't thought the outlaw to be that smart. Because of Paul's carelessness, this "Kid" had managed to reach Elsie in the Native camp, where she was supposed to be safe. It would take time for her to get past what had happened.

They had made it through another fight, though, and that counted for something.

"Come on." He stood and offered her his hand. "Let's get you cleaned up."

She hesitated, her eyes lingering on his hand before she finally took it. He pulled her up carefully, holding her steady as she got to her feet. For a moment, they stood there, close enough that her warmth radiated against Paul, and her breath touched his face.

He nodded toward the camp. "We'll take it slow. No rush."

Elsie gave him a small, grateful smile, and her fingers tightening around. "Thanks, Paul."

"Always, Elsie. Always."

198

Chapter Twenty-Four

30 miles south of Wichita

The morning dawned crisp, and Elsie shivered as she wrapped her faded woolen shawl tighter around her shoulders.

The frosty air nipped at her skin, reminding her that autumn in Indian territory could be unforgiving. She readied herself to leave the safety of the Cherokee camp, grateful for the time they'd spent here. The tribe had treated them well, offering warmth, food, and supplies to sustain them, but more than anything, it was their understanding that gave Elsie comfort. They seemed to recognize what Jon was—without her needing to explain—a small but much-needed validation.

She hadn't expected them to offer weapons—bowie knives with carved bone handles—and an escort for the first ten miles of their journey, so when Marcus translated the offer, she was more than grateful.

The truth was, knowing they'd have a tribal escort flanking them on their painted ponies gave her a comfort she wouldn't admit out loud. She knew how Jon feared Natives, especially since the Frontier Wars had been ravaging settlers' minds with stories of raids and ambushes. Jon had always made a show of dismissing them as "savages," but Elsie could see through his bravado. It was one more barrier between her and his grasping hands.

As they prepared to leave, Rocco and Jody approached Elsie, their rough, trail-beaten hats held respectfully in their hands.

"Reckon we'll stick it out here." Rocco rubbed the back of his head, avoiding eye contact. "Too much excitement for us, you get?"

Jody nodded. "Ain't nothin' personal, Elsie. We're just not built for the kind of trouble that's doggin' ya."

Elsie tried to smile, but it felt forced. She couldn't blame them for wanting to stay behind, especially since they'd already suffered so much because of Jon's obsession with her. She appreciated their honesty, even if it hurt with a hollow ache that had nothing to do with fear or exhaustion.

She told them so and bid them farewell, giving each of them a brief, sincere hug before they turned back toward the camp.

When the time came, Cherokee scouts led the way ahead of them, rifles slung over their shoulders, beads and feathers adorning their vests. Elsie rode beside Paul, among the soft clink of bridles and the crunch of hooves over uneven earth. Paul glanced her way now and then, as if gauging her mood, his brow furrowed in that way she'd come to find both comforting and frustrating. He wore his weathered Stetson, one that must have seen countless dusty cattle drives from Texas to Dodge City.

He'd stepped in to save her again and again, without question or reservation—both physically and emotionally—dragging her out of the Washita when she'd misjudged the crossing and nearly drowned, giving her time to find her peace yesterday, after Kid almost ran off with her. The way he acted around her, always ready to help, both warmed and terrified her. It was getting harder not to acknowledge the feelings blooming inside her, and she wasn't sure she could ignore them much longer.

"Got any ideas what we can do 'bout Jon?" Paul frowned as he looked ahead. "He's been real slippery so far."

She shook her head slowly. "I don't reckon there's much we can do. We can't go after him, and he'll find me wherever I go."

Marcus's deep voice chimed in. "What if he didn't have the right to come after ya?"

Elsie gave him a confused look.

"I have a friend," Marcus said, rubbing his gray stubble. "Left her husband back in '67, right after the war. He'd been abusive, and the judge said she had the right to leave. Didn't have to stay no more."

Elsie blinked. The words were almost incomprehensible at first. "A judge said that?" A tiny spark of hope flickered in her chest, something she hadn't dared feel for so long. "I... Jon always kept me alone and isolated, but—If you say a judge said it..."

"Might take some convincin', but it's possible." Marcus nodded solemnly, his eyes narrowing against the rising sun. "Things are changin'."

For the first time in years, Elsie let herself imagine freedom—real freedom. No more hiding, no more running. She thought of Wichita, the growing rail town, where the courts might offer her a chance. She could go to a judge, could be free

But even divorced, Jon could still come after her. He could still hunt her down, could still ruin whatever new life she tried to make for herself.

"Even if I leave him..." She looked down at the reins clutched in her hands, her fingers cold despite the sun climbing higher. "Jon wouldn't just let me go. He'll come after me. He'll always come after me."

Marcus rode closer, his horse sidling up beside hers. He leaned in, his voice low. "Elsie, you gotta understand. Jon's just a man. Ain't no demon. If he's comin' for ya, well, he's gotta get through us first. You ain't alone in this."

"Thank you, Marcus." She shuddered and took a deep breath. "Reckon I just ain't used to havin' folks on my side."

Marcus smiled. "Well, you best get used to it. We're in this together, and we don't leave our own behind. Not on my watch."

"What if you weren't alone, Elsie?" Paul's voice was uncharacteristically soft. "What if you had someone by your side—someone he couldn't just bully or threaten?"

Elsie turned to look at him, her heart giving a strange, unexpected lurch.

"I could marry you. In Wichita." He spoke the words so casually, as if he hadn't just offered to change her world. "I've sent him runnin' several times now. He'd think twice before comin' after you if you were my wife."

Her heart thundered louder than the hoofbeats that echoed around them.

Confusion and warmth bloomed within her chest and fought against her instinct to push everyone away. She hadn't allowed herself to feel much for Paul beyond the bond of survival, but the feelings had grown, nonetheless. Now, everything she'd been ignoring about him—his steady strength, his quiet kindness, the way he always seemed to notice when she was struggling—hit her all at once. She cared for him.

Perhaps more deeply than she wanted to admit.

She remembered the first time Paul had really looked at her—not as a trail hand, but as a person. It had been during the fight with the soldiers at Fort Reno, when he'd seen her holding her ground, fighting like hell to keep the camp safe. His eyes had flicked to hers afterward, something in them shifting, something that made her wonder if maybe he saw through her disguise more clearly than she'd thought. He hadn't called her out on it. Instead, he had simply stood beside her, a quiet shield, making sure she was alright.

But it wouldn't be fair to him. Not with the mess she carried. He deserved better. He deserved someone who wasn't a target, someone who wasn't constantly looking over her shoulder for shadows in the night.

"Paul, I—" She tried to find the words, tried to tell him that he shouldn't have to do this, that she wasn't worth the risk.

"You're worth more than you think, Elsie." His eyes locked onto hers. "I know you think you have to carry all this alone, but you don't. You don't have to keep runnin' forever. You deserve a chance to live without lookin' over your shoulder."

Her throat tightened, and her vision blurred as she looked at him. She swallowed hard, trying to steady herself. " But I'll just drag you into my mess. Jon won't stop, no matter how many times he failed to kill you before."

"Don't you worry 'bout me. I've faced worse men than him, and I'd do it again if it meant keepin' you safe." He paused, and his expression grew serious. "I know you're scared. I'd be a fool not to understand that. But I'm not offerin' this lightly. I—"

Before he could finish the thought, the Cherokee at the front of their group raised his hand, signaling for a halt.

The escort had reached the end of their journey with them.

Each Cherokee in their escort offered a firm handshake or a nod of farewell. Elsie bowed her head, and a lump formed in her throat. Gratitude. Fear. Hope. So many emotions tangled inside her, none of them clear.

She thought of the woman who'd sat with her the night before, speaking softly in her native tongue, holding Elsie's hands between her own. Though Elsie hadn't understood the words, their warmth had seeped into her, giving her courage she'd almost forgotten she could feel.

Marcus put his hand on her shoulder as they watched the Natives ride off. "You did good, Elsie. These folks see the strength in ya, same as we do. Don't forget that."

"Thanks, Marcus."

They rode on, and Elsie tried to imagine what a life with Paul would look like.

She imagined the ranch he'd spoken of, half-burned, then rebuilt. She imagined herself helping to mend fences, working with cattle, feeling Paul's steady presence beside her. She thought about nights spent under the stars, not as Eli, the trail hand, but as Elsie, truly herself, with no more lies between them. Ever.

It was a picture so different from anything she'd allowed herself to imagine before. It scared her as much as it gave her hope. Did she deserve happiness like that? What if something took it away from her in the end?

She didn't think she could handle that.

Paul's voice broke through her thoughts. "What are you thinkin' on?"

Elsie blinked, then looked at him, a soft smile touching her lips. "I'm thinkin' maybe I could be brave enough. Maybe."

"That's all I ask. Just think on it."

Marcus, who'd been riding a few paces behind, chimed in, his voice carrying a teasing note. "Thinking's fine and all, but just so you two know, we've still got cattle to drive. I don't plan on doin' all the work myself."

"Don't you worry, old man." Paul let out a low chuckle. "Ain't nobody trust you to do anything alone, nohow."

"We'd better pick up the pace." Elsie winked at him. "I think you just gave Marcus an excuse to slack off."

"Damn right he did." Marcus tipped his hat over his milky eye. "If I'm old, I'm restin!"

"That ain't flyin' with me around, grandpa!" She giggled. "You got some life left in you yet."

For the first time in a long while, the fear in her chest seemed to loosen its hold. She wasn't sure what lay ahead, but maybe—just maybe—she wouldn't have to face it alone. If she took that chance.

They had two days left to Wichita—two days to figure out if she could be brave enough to believe in a different future.

Chapter Twenty-Five

Wichita

Paul didn't much like the look the sheriff gave him as they walked into the small office.

The room smelled of old leather and tobacco. Worn floorboards creaked under their boots, wide, scuffed planks that had seen years of heavy wear. The sheriff's desk was cluttered with wanted posters, tin mugs, and a brass oil lamp that flickered in the dim light.

Elsie kept her eyes downcast, fingers trembling as they rested on her lap. She'd been quiet ever since they dismounted outside the sheriff's place, and that silence worried Paul more than any words she could've said.

He'd promised himself to keep her safe, and it tore at him that there were battles he couldn't simply fight for her.

The sheriff, a grizzled man with a face like worn leather called Bill Kane, leaned back in his chair, squinting at them from under a wide-brimmed hat. His chair creaked as he rocked slowly, giving Elsie a long, hard look. His unbuttoned vest revealed a yellowed shirt, patched up more times than it was surely worth, and a pocket watch that glinted faintly in the lamplight.

"So, let me get this straight." He scratched the side of his jaw. "You want me to believe you're Elsie Wadsworth, wife of one Jonathan Rickett? The same Big Jon Rickett who's got half of San Antonio too scared to even say his name?"

"Yes, sir." Elsie swallowed hard, gripping the worn hat in her hands like it was the only thing keeping her steady. "I'm her. I've been trying to get away from him for years."

"Well, Miss Wadsworth... or whatever your name is, I don't know if you're aware, but plenty of people have tried to use the name of one outlaw or another to gain sympathy or cover their tracks." He tilted his head back. "Hard to believe you're really his wife when you're standin' here, askin' for an annulment like it's a simple matter."

Elsie reached into her coat with shaky fingers and pulled out a folded piece of paper. She unfolded it to show Paul a wanted poster, crumpled and yellowed at the edges. The corners of the poster were torn, the ink smeared, but Elsie's face was sketched on it, clear as day—younger and with a wilder look in her eyes, but unmistakably her.

She handed it over without a word.

Sheriff Kane stared at the poster, then back at Elsie, and frowned.

"Well, I'll be damned." He sat up straight, his incredulity shifting into genuine surprise. He glanced at the date stamped on the bottom—*1871*. "This really is you, ain't it?"

Elsie nodded again, her cheeks flushing. She bit her lip and stared at the floor. Paul had seen that look before—the weight of the past hanging heavy, even when it wasn't your fault.

Paul stepped closer, putting a hand on her shoulder. The way she seemed to shrink inward only fueled his frustration.

If he could carry the weight of her past on his own back, he would.

"With what they say 'bout Rickett, I've no doubt you didn't earn that wanted poster on your own merit. But I gotta say, you got yourself tied up with one hell of a mess." Sheriff Kane folded the poster carefully and set it on his desk. "But that don't mean I can just wave a hand and annul your marriage. I'll need to reach out to a judge."

They'd known that before they came in here, but the way Elsie's jaw clenched made Paul's chest pang. He knew she didn't want to be in Wichita any longer than necessary—none of them did.

He looked at the sheriff. "How long will it take?"

"The closest judge is in Leoti, but that's more than two hundred miles away. I'll try to reach them via telegram, but it could be a few days, regardless." He glanced at Elsie with a look that carried both understanding and wariness. "You two best stay low. Wichita's quiet, but folks love to talk."

Paul squeezed Elsie's shoulder. "We'll wait."

Sheriff Kane grunted. "Ain't got much choice in the matter. You can stay at the boarding house down the way."

Paul nodded, and they walked out of the sheriff's office.

Wagon wheels and hooves churned on the dirt road that stretched before them. Paul's muscles ached as they walked—too many days in the saddle, too many sleepless nights. The town was a mix of old wood and newer constructions, false-front buildings with faded signs advertising dry goods, a blacksmith, and a saloon.

Marcus and Wohali were waiting just outside town with the herd, but they'd have to wait until tomorrow for the delivery. Elsie was too high-strung right now, and Paul intended to give her the time to rest and get her nerves sorted. Besides,

Wohali was used to sleeping in the wild, and Marcus was a hardened trail hand.

One more day in a bedroll wouldn't hurt them.

Paul scanned the street as he and Elsie walked toward the edge of the town, where the sheriff had told them the boarding house was. Jon hadn't reared his ugly head in the past two days, but that was no reason to lower their guard now. Paul kept his stride even, his eyes sharp for anything out of place.

That a habit had kept him alive all these years.

The air was thick with the scent of sweat, leather, and dust. The clatter of a horse-drawn wagon rolled past, the driver flicking the reins with a worn leather glove. Every stranger's glance was a potential threat, and Paul couldn't shake the feeling that someone was watching.

A woman dressed finer than most, with a bustled dress and parasol, eyed him up and down as they passed. She smiled, giving him a once-over that made his skin crawl. He increased his pace, pulling Elsie along with him. The chances that the woman was working with Jon's gang were low, but he still wanted to get out of her sight as quickly as possible.

His hand lingered at the small of Elsie's back, guiding her along, and he felt the way her body tensed at the contact. He understood that tension—she'd been through hell, and touch wasn't always a comfort.

But she didn't pull away either, and that, in some small way, felt like a step forward.

They reached the boarding house—a sagging two-story building with peeling paint and a weary-looking innkeeper sitting on the porch. The sign above the door, *Greenwood Boarding House,* swung slightly in the breeze, its letters faded and chipped. Paul negotiated a room for him and Elsie with the man and led Elsie back outside.

He needed to tell Marcus and Wohali, who were staying outside the town to keep an eye on the herd, about the change of plans.

Elsie faltered beside him. "I'm sorry." Her voice was soft and full of guilt. "I'm draggin' you down."

Paul stopped walking and turned to face her. Her eyes were down, as if she couldn't bear to look at him.

He frowned. "What are you talkin' about?"

"That woman. She looked at you like—like I'm standing in the way. Maybe I am." Elsie bit her lip. "You deserve better. A real life, not one spent hiding or fixing someone else's mess."

Paul stared at her, his heart pounding with things he hadn't said yet. Things he wasn't sure how to say. Here she was, thinking she was a burden, when all he wanted was to keep her safe. He reached out, gently tipping her chin up so she'd look at him.

Her eyes met his, and in them, Paul saw the storm of emotions—fear, doubt, and something else, something raw and vulnerable that she kept buried beneath all those layers of pain. He didn't know how to make her understand how he felt, but he knew he had to try. He couldn't let her keep thinking she was dragging him down.

"I ain't goin' anywhere, Elsie. I'm right where I want to be."

Her eyes searched his, confusion and doubt swirling in them. "But... you could have something else. Someone else. A woman like her, maybe. Not—"

"Not what?" He smiled, his voice softening. "Not a woman who's stronger than half the men I've met? Not someone who's been through hell and come out the other side still fighting?"

He paused, letting his words settle between them. He could see her struggling to believe it, her gaze flickering away, her lip caught between her teeth.

"But—"

"No, Elsie." He shook his head, trying to find the right words. "I've cared for you for longer than I've let on. You ain't keepin' me from happiness. You *are* my happiness."

Her lips parted in surprise, and for a moment, neither of them moved.

Tears gathered at the edges of her eyes, and his heart ached at the sight. He knew she wasn't used to anyone standing by her side without expecting something in return. Jon had taught her to expect pain and abandonment, and Paul wanted to be the one to prove that wrong.

She reached out and clasped his hand. Her skin was warm, rough from the trail but soft against his own. His thumb brushed over the back of her hand, a promise of everything he hadn't yet said.

"If you'll have me," he murmured, his voice low and earnest, "I like the idea of bein' your husband."

Elsie blinked, tears gathering at the edges of her eyes, but she smiled—a small, fragile thing, but real.

"Paul..." She squeezed his hand, her voice trembling. "I would."

For a moment, they stood there, hands entwined, the world around them fading into nothing but the quiet connection between them. Paul felt the tension ease from his chest, the uncertainty that had gripped him for so long finally loosening its hold.

This was what he wanted—this woman, this life, whatever came with it.

Paul looked past her, toward the horizon, where the train tracks lay as a stark reminder of the changing times and the iron beast that would soon put men like him out of work. He knew it wasn't over yet. Jon Rickett was still out there, and getting rid of him would be far from easy.

He was fighting for Elsie, though, and no enemy seemed daunting.

Chapter Twenty-Six

Wichita

As Paul guided the herd into the market, the rhythm of the cattle's hooves echoed in his bones, and the sight of the corral brought a grim satisfaction. This was the final stretch, the last responsibility they had before dividing the profit.

The end of the cattle trails, too, though the thought didn't bother Paul as much as it had before.

Paul exchanged a glance with Elsie, her hat pulled low, her eyes sharp as ever.

Soon enough, Aldo's buyer showed up, a stout man, chewing tobacco and nodding as he surveyed the herd. Paul kept his words direct and negotiated with the same calm pragmatism he'd used to keep the herd together. Aldo had already made a deal, but he wasn't here. This was Paul's last drive, and he was going to get everyone a bit more money for all the trouble they'd gone through, Aldo be damned.

The buyer moaned about Aldo and the deal, of course, but his body language screamed the truth at Paul: he *needed* the cattle, and he would pay more to get them. Eventually, the buyer spat a glob of red saliva into the dust and agreed to Paul's price.

He handed over the money and left with the cattle.

The bills were worn, creased from the grasp of countless hands. It wasn't like the money you'd find in a bank—this was trail money, grimy and hard-earned, just like everything else in Paul's life. He could smell the faint mix of tobacco and sweat that clung to the bills, a reminder of where they came from and the lives they had touched.

Paul quietly set Aldo's share apart and split the remaining between himself, Elsie, Marcus, and Wohali. He even set apart a share for Rocco and Jody. They'd stayed in the Cherokee camp, but they had been good trail hands up until that point.

"Please take this to them." He spoke in Wohali's language as he handed the Cherokee youth Rocco and Jody's share. "And thank you. For everything."

"Take care, Paul Boone." Wohali nodded. "May your journey with Elsie be a good one."

Warmth spread through Paul's chest as Wohali turned away and faded slowly into the crowded Wichita street. Paul *was* about to embark on a journey—a life with Elsie, or so he hoped—and the thought was encouraging. What the two of them had was more than infatuation or a relationship born of idle town courtship. It was a bond forged through the hard miles of the Chisholm Trail behind them.

If she'd still have him, of course.

Paul lingered for a moment, staring down the street after Wohali. He couldn't help but think about how the youth was going back to his people, to his tribe, and it struck Paul that everyone had somewhere they belonged—everyone except him. For the first time in a long while, though, Paul felt a sense of hope that he might have found that place with Elsie.

"Don't know 'bout the rest of you, but I'm headin' to the saloon." Marcus pocketed his share of the pay with a grin. "Think I've earned myself an afternoon of doin' nothin'."

Paul shook his hand. "You've earned that and more, my friend."

Marcus tipped his hat to Elsie. "You two take care now." With that, he ambled off, his gait loose.

The street was bustling, filled with wagons rattling over the uneven planks of the wooden sidewalks, the wheels creaking loudly. Horses tied to hitching posts snorted and shifted, their tails flicking at flies, while men in broad Stetsons and dusty coats moved in and out of the buildings lining the street. The pungent smell of horse manure mixed with wood smoke, and the distant hiss of a blacksmith's forge filled the air, grounding Paul in the reality of this town.

It was the smell of change, of civilization pushing its way west.

Moments later, Sheriff Kane found them. His approach was unmistakable, the jangle of his spurs echoing through the dusty street.

"Boone!" he called, raising a hand.

Paul turned and raised an eyebrow at the sheriff's pleased expression.

"Telegraph came in." The sheriff gave Elsie a nod before continuing. "Judge allowed the annulment on the grounds of cruelty. It's already filed back in Leoti."

Paul's chest loosened at the words. He glanced at Elsie, whose lips parted in a sigh that seemed to carry years of weight.

Paul clasped the man's hand. "Thank you, sheriff."

Sheriff Kane tipped his hat. "Figured you'd want to get that news sooner than later. Good luck to you both, and let me know if you learn anything about Rickett's whereabouts."

He gave them a curt nod before turning away and leaving them standing there.

Paul looked at Elsie. "Head to the church with me? No sense waitin'."

Elsie blinked up at him, and a smile bloomed on her lips. "Alright."

They made their way down the packed dirt of the road, but Paul's insecurities crawled their way out from the depths of his subconscious with each step he took. Memories of Katherine and the letter she'd left, telling him that she needed an easier life than he could give her. Elsie was stronger than Katherine could ever hope to be, but the truth remained the same.

Paul could only ever give her a life on a ranch.

Paul's mind churned as they walked, memories flashing of his father, the war, and the empty ranch he'd struggled to keep. All the losses he'd carried over the years stacked up in his mind like weights on his back. He remembered how it felt to come home after the war, to see the ruins of everything he'd once hoped to build, and the realization that no one was waiting for him. He didn't want to go through that again—not with Elsie.

"You know, Elsie..." He gulped and stared down. "You don't have to do this. You can have a better life than a ranch. A better man than me."

She'd come so far since the day they'd met that day at the Washita, when she'd nearly drowned. Back then, she'd been nervous, unsure. She'd tried so hard to keep her secret and prove herself as "Eli." Now, she was standing beside him, ready to face whatever came their way, no longer hiding who she was. It struck Paul deeply just how much courage it had taken for Elsie to transform from the frightened trail scout to the determined woman she was now.

It made him want to protect her all the more, even from potentially wasting her life on him.

Elsie stopped him in his tracks and pushed his chin up. There was no hesitation in her gaze, just a steady, determined warmth. She stepped closer, her fingers brushing against his arm. "I don't want a better man, Paul. I want you. I want this life—whatever it is—as long as it's with you."

Paul swallowed hard. "Alright... Then we better stop at the saloon first."

"What?"

He smiled. "Trust me."

They made their way to the saloon. It was dimly lit, with a few flickering oil lamps casting long shadows against the worn wooden walls. Sawdust covered the floor, meant to soak up spills, and the sharp tang of whiskey mixed with the ever-present odors of sweat and tobacco. The sound of an out-of-tune piano tinkling away in the corner added to the chaotic charm of the place.

Marcus was nursing a drink, a relaxed grin on his face.

"Marcus!" Paul called.

Marcus looked up, surprise flickering across his features. "Paul? Why aren't you at the church?"

"Need you to be my best man!"

Marcus blinked, then set down his drink, stood up, and slammed a few coins on the counter. "Well, I'll be damned! I'd be honored."

Paul felt a surge of gratitude for Marcus. During all the miles they'd ridden, all the dangers they'd faced, Marcus had been there, a steady presence. Paul knew he couldn't do this without him. Marcus had become more than just a companion on the trail—he'd become a true friend, and Paul wanted him by his side for this moment.

The trio made their way to the church. Paul felt a happiness unlike any he'd known before as they approached the wooden building. For a moment, everything felt right. Paul allowed himself to think of the future. He imagined himself and Elsie on the ranch, working side by side. He saw them tending to the animals together, sharing quiet evenings on the porch, maybe even raising a family. The image was so vivid, so real, that it made his heart swell. He wanted that future more than anything, and he knew Elsie did too. It wasn't the life of ease Katherine had wanted, but it was a life filled with love and purpose—and that was worth fighting for.

Then he saw them.

Jon and the remaining members of his gang stood in front of the church, their faces hard, eyes locked on Paul and Elsie.

Paul instinctively reached for the revolver at his side, and Elsie grabbed her own. Marcus took up his rifle.

"Well, well, well." Jon's gaze flicked to Elsie, a twisted smile curving his lips. "You've brought me my wife back, Boone. To show you how grateful I am, I'll let you watch us renew our vows. This time, we're going to add a part about not escaping your loving husband."

Paul's mind sharpened, each detail coming into focus. He noted the way Jon's fingers twitched near his belt, the restless shifting of the men at Jon's back. They were tense, unpredictable, and Paul knew that one wrong move could set them off. He remembered the war, the way he'd learned to read a man's body language—how desperation showed itself in the smallest of gestures.

Jon was desperate, and that made him dangerous.

"Jon Rickett, Elsie ain't your possession. She never was, and she never will be." Paul's jaw tightened, and his muscles tensed as he stepped in front of Elsie. "You got no claim here."

Paul's eyes darted, searching for any advantage—a place to take cover, a way to draw Jon's men away from Elsie and Marcus. He could feel the tension radiating from Elsie, her palpable determination. He knew she wouldn't back down, and neither would he.

This was their moment—everything they had fought for, everything they had endured—came down to this.

Jon raised his pistol.

Chapter Twenty-Seven

Wichita

Elsie's heart pounded in her chest as the gunfight erupted, and the initial explosion of sound ripped through the street.

She crouched behind a stack of wooden crates, her revolver clutched tightly, eyes darting frantically as she took in the chaotic scene unfolding around her. Paul was positioned to her right, using an overturned cart as cover, and Marcus knelt behind a barrel next to her left. Elsie's pulse thrummed in her ears, perfectly in tune with the deafening roar of gunfire. The acrid scent of gunpowder, mixed with the dust kicked up by dozens of hurried footsteps, was thick enough to taste.

Jon and his men were scattered, using anything they could find for cover.

Jon skulked behind a broken-down wagon. Raymond, a tall and gaunt man with a hawklike appearance who wore a faded black duster, and Little Ben, short and stocky with a round face and a perpetual sneer, crouched behind some barrels. Kid Olsen and Layton hunkered down behind an overturned market stall, peeking out occasionally to take shots at anyone they could see.

Elsie fired with Paul and Marcus, but the difference in numbers was starting to show. Elsie's group had no one to pit against Raymond and Little Ben. Jon's gang hadn't been able to emerge from their cover yet, but they soon would. At that point, the gang would outflank their little group and gun Paul and Marcus down. They would be gone, just like Fannie.

Then, Jon would take her back.

The thought of Jon capturing her again twisted a knot in her gut, memories of his bruising grip and cold sneer flashing behind her eyes. She squeezed the handle of her revolver tightly, knowing this wasn't just another fight—it was her last chance to escape the cage he'd built around her life.

She couldn't go back. She wouldn't, especially now that she had a life with Paul to look forward to. She'd be damned if she let Jon take that future away from her.

Her ears rang from the crack of gunfire, and every shot felt like it reverberated through her bones. The dust choked her, the heat of the sun adding to the suffocating sensation of the fight closing in around her.

Two more guns joined the fray, and Elsie exhaled.

Sheriff Kane and his deputy took position behind a nearby building and fired on the outlaws. Shouts mixed with the thunder of revolvers being fired again and again. The street was a disorienting swirl of dust, smoke, and jarring violence. Every movement seemed like a blur, her vision filled with fleeting images of flashing muzzles, darting shadows, and the dull glint of weapons in the sunlight.

Paul broke his cover without warning and charged at Jon with long strides.

Elsie's heart leapt into her throat. It was suicide. The open stretch of ground Paul was running across was impossibly long, and each step he took could be his last. Her breath caught, and for a split second, all she wanted to do was scream for him to come back—but he was already committed, and she couldn't let him down.

She held her breath and stood up to lay down covering fire at one outlaws after another. Her fingers trembled as she aimed—every shot had to count. Her body shook with the effort of holding steady, her mind battling against the frantic voice screaming that she was about to lose everything.

She had to focus and give Paul time to cross the kill zone. Even if she got hurt—even if she got killed—if she could give him a single second without them firing at him, it would be worth it.

Jon turned, his eyes widening as he saw Paul bearing down on him, but it was too late. Paul reached him and tackled him hard.

Both men went down, rolling in the dust, and Paul descended on Jon with a flurry of punches. The dirt they kicked up made it impossible to see them, but Elsie had no doubt Paul would have the upper hand.

He had to.

Still, she had her own worries right now. Marcus was firing at Kid and Layton from behind his barrel, and Elsie shifted her position to support him. They fired in tandem, breaking Kid and Layton's market stall one piece of wood at a time.

Sheriff Kane and his deputy were pressing forward, their focus on Raymond and Little Ben. The two outlaws took hasty shots in an attempt to hold the lawmen back, but the lawmen closed the distance carefully, without leaving an opening.

A sharp cry tore through the chaos next to her, distinct even above the roar of gunfire. Elsie's head snapped toward Marcus, and her breath caught in her throat. He'd been hit.

Blood soaked through his pants, the color draining from his face as he struggled to remain upright. He gritted his teeth, one hand pressed against the wound to slow the bleeding.

"Marcus!" She fired blindly in Kid and Layton's direction.

He met her gaze and shook his head, grimacing as he waved her off.

Her heart ached seeing him like that—vulnerable and hurt—but she knew he was right. They couldn't afford to let up, not now. There was no room for weakness, not when everything was on the line.

She forced herself to turn back to the fight, her eyes scanning for a target.

Kid and Layton had moved while she was distracted with Marcus, and she couldn't find them. Raymond, however, had his back turned to her as he fired toward the sheriff.

Elsie took a deep breath, willing her hands to stay steady. She curled her finger around the trigger, the world narrowing to just her and her target. The shot rang out.

Raymond jerked, his body stiffening, before he collapsed into the dust. Elsie let out a shaky breath of relief, but her throat closed when she turned to her right.

Kid Olson stood mere steps away, and the barrel of his pistol was pointed right between her eyes.

Her stomach dropped, her body freezing as she met his cold gaze. His finger was tightening on the trigger, and there was nothing she could do about it. This was it. Her heart pounded in her ears, drowning out the noise around her. She was about to die at the hand of *Kid Olson*.

Fury laced her fear. Anger at herself for letting her guard down. At Kid, for being Jon's pawn and an awful, cruel excuse for a human being. At Jon, for everything he'd taken from her.

In the seconds it was taking Kid to shoot her, she stared at him with defiance, unwilling to give him the satisfaction of seeing her break, even as she knew she was seconds from death.

She flinched as the shot rang out, then blinked with confusion when the pain didn't come.

Kid's eyes widened, his expression shifting to one of shock. His body went slack, his revolver falling from his hand, and he crumpled to the ground. As he fell, Layton stood revealed, smoke curling from his revolver, his face set in a grim mask.

Time seemed to stand still as Elsie stared at Layton, struggling to comprehend what had just happened. Layton—Jon's right-hand man—had turned on his own.

Their eyes met, and for a fleeting second, she saw something in his gaze—a silent acknowledgment, an understanding of the choices they had all been forced to make. He gave her a curt nod, and then he was gone, sprinting down a narrow alley and disappearing from sight.

His act of betrayal had saved her life, and she didn't know how to feel about that.

In that moment, she realized the price of all their choices—the lines they were forced to cross. Was this how far they had fallen? To the point where even Jon's men, bound by loyalty and violence, would break their own rules to survive? She wasn't sure whether to feel grateful or disgusted. In another life, Layton might have been an ally—or maybe someone just as broken as she herself had once been.

But there was no time to think about it now.

Elsie forced her attention back to the fight, her eyes searching for Paul. She found him and Jon still locked in their struggle, rolling in the dirt, each trying to overpower the other. With Kid and Raymond dead, Marcus wounded, and Layton gone, only Little Ben and the two lawmen kept firing.

Between the sporadic shots, Elsie heard Paul and Jon's grunts and the dull thud of fists landing on flesh.

Paul's face was twisted in concentration, his muscles straining as he fought to keep Jon down. Jon managed to get a hand around Paul's throat, his fingers digging in, but Paul swung his arm, knocking his grip loose. He pushed Jon down, his weight pressing against him, his hands moving to Jon's neck.

Elsie's heart pounded painfully as she watched, her breath catching in her throat.

Paul's expression hardened, his eyes narrowing with determination. With a final, brutal twist and a sickening crack, Jon's body went limp, his neck broken.

It was over.

Jon was dead, his control over her shattered in the same brutal way Paul had ended his life. The weight she'd carried for years—the fear, the pain, the chains he'd wrapped around her heart—lifted in a single, shuddering breath. She felt hollow and full all at once, like she could finally breathe, yet couldn't stop trembling.

The man who'd stolen everything from her was gone, and for the first time, she felt truly free. However, freedom didn't feel like the victory she'd imagined—it felt fragile, like it could slip away with the wind.

Paul.

She needed Paul.

Her legs shook as she pushed herself off the ground, dust clinging to her clothes, mixing with the damp sweat that streaked her skin. She holstered her revolver with trembling hands, her gaze locked on Paul and the lifeless form at his feet. Her heart was still racing, not from the danger that had passed, but from the sight of Paul—alive, strong, and unshaken by the violence he'd just unleashed.

He was *alive.*

Paul knelt there, chest heaving, his fists still clenched, staring down at Jon as if daring him to rise again.

Elsie swallowed against the tightness in her throat and took a step toward him. "Paul?"

He stared at Jon's body as if the rage hadn't fully left him. As if he hadn't processed that the fight was over. Then, after a long breath, his head turned slightly, and his gaze found hers.

She crossed the distance and knelt next to him. "Paul." She took his hand in hers.

"He's gone." Paul muttered. "You're free now. For good."

Elsie nodded, tears stinging her eyes, though they weren't tears of sadness or fear. These were tears of relief, of release, of the kind of love she hadn't known she could feel until this man had shown her what it meant to be cherished.

"So are you," she whispered, her voice breaking just slightly.

Paul looked at her, confusion flickering across his face. "What?"

"You're free." She reached up to cradle his face and brushed her thumbs against the rough edge of his beard. "Free from all the ghosts you think you're still running from. From all the things you think make you less than you are. None of that matters to me, Paul. None of it."

Paul's hands, calloused from the trail and stained from the fight, found her waist and pulled her close, as if grounding himself in her presence. "I just don't want you to have any regrets about... being with me."

"Paul, look at me." She tried to force all her feelings for him into the look she was giving him. "There's no one in this world for me but you. *No one.* You've shown me how to be strong. You've never given up on me, and you've saved me more times than I can count—not just from Jon, from myself as well. From the fear, the doubt... from thinking I wasn't worth saving."

Paul's grip on her tightened. "Elsie..."

"I'm yours, Paul," she whispered, threading her fingers through his hair. "And you're mine."

"I..." Paul leaned in and pressed his lips against her forehead. "I love you."

"I love you too, Paul."

Chapter Twenty-Eight

Wichita

After all the fuss about the gunfight two days ago had ended, Paul and Elsie were able to get married in peace, and Paul was glad to be able to relax for once.

The feeling of constantly watching his back, of being ready to draw at a moment's notice, had been his reality for so long that this calmness felt foreign, almost unsettling. But with Elsie beside him, he allowed himself to breathe, to let go of the weight he'd carried for years. It was a small taste of what peace could be—something he hadn't dared dream about since before the war.

He was sitting in the board house parlor with Elsie by his side. The fire crackled in the hearth, casting a warm glow across the room, and outside, the distant sounds of Federal soldiers moving about reminded him that Layton was still on the run.

A part of him wanted to help track the man down, but Elsie had asked him not to—out of gratitude for the way Layton had treated her with respect while she'd been with Jon, even when things had turned dangerous. Besides, the man had killed one of his own to spare her life.

"You think he'll really get away?" Paul turned his head toward her.

"Who?" She was staring into the fire, the orange light reflecting in her eyes. "Layton?"

"Yeah."

She shrugged, leaning into his shoulder. "He's always been a slippery one. He'll make it back home just fine."

"If you say so."

"We should head to the clinic." Elsie nuzzled into him. "Check on Marcus."

Paul stood first, offering her his hand, a gesture as natural as breathing now. It struck him how far he'd come—from a man who kept his heart locked away, avoiding any emotional ties, to someone who now craved the closeness of another. For so long, solitude had been his shield, keeping him safe from the pain of loss.

But Elsie had broken through that, and now, here he was, reaching out for her without hesitation. It felt good—like a piece of himself had finally come home.

He still couldn't quite wrap his head around it—being married, being this close to someone. After years of solitude, it was strange, but good.

They made their way through the streets of Wichita. Shopkeepers called out prices for bolts of fabric, tin tools, and sacks of dried beans as they passed, and children ran along the dusty streets, their laughter mixing with the clattering of horses' hooves. The air was filled with the rich scent of fresh-baked bread from the bakery, mingling with the earthy smell of hay and the faint tang of horse sweat. The warmth of the late afternoon sun settled over everything, giving the town a vibrant, almost nostalgic feel.

It was a lively town, and Paul was almost sad to leave it for his broken ranch.

Almost.

The clinic smelled of carbolic acid and chamomile, a mix of sharp antiseptic and soothing herbs. Marcus sat on the bed, looking impossibly calm for a man who'd been through the Chisholm Trail and then shot through the leg. His hat was propped up beside him, and he was fiddling with a small carving knife, whittling a piece of wood into some vague shape.

He gave them a small nod as they entered.

"Marcus," Elsie smiled, crossing the room quickly. "How are you feeling?"

"Never better." Marcus's one good eye twinkled. "It's going to take more than a bullet in the leg to do in me. Especially with you two alright."

"I still want you restin'." She chuckled. "You're already the one-eyed man, no need to be the one-*legged* one."

Marcus laughed. "Don't you worry 'bout me. You got your partner now, and you two make quite a team."

Elsie blushed, brushing a loose strand of hair behind her ear. "Thank you, Marcus."

"Oh, don't you get all emotional on me, now."

"I mean it." She spoke more quietly. "Thank you for everything. For keeping my secret, for helping us along the way. I don't know how we would've made it without you."

"Don't you mention it. I needed one last adventure before settling down—and this was a hell of an adventure!" He leaned back and steepled his fingers behind his head. "But I think it's high time I retired. I'm staying here in Wichita. I figure I've earned a bit of rest."

Elsie's eyes widened. "You're staying?"

"The cattle trails are done, and even if they weren't, the wilderness is no place for an old dog like me. Don't you worry, though." He winked at her. "I'll be around if you need me."

Paul nodded at Marcus, and Marcus nodded back. They didn't need to speak about it. Yes, Paul was more than sad that Marcus would stay in Wichita and likely never leave and never see Paul and Elsie again. Not unless the two of them came to Wichita to visit.

Still, the man had earned his peace.

They stayed for a while longer, talking and laughing in a way that felt rare and precious. Marcus told them stories about his earlier days, about places he'd been and people he'd met. His voice held a note of nostalgia, and Paul found himself listening more intently than he'd expected, taking in every detail. Elsie was just as absorbed, her eyes wide as Marcus spoke of a time before the war, of friends long gone and trails that stretched out endlessly under the sky.

It was as if time had slowed down, allowing them to savor the connection they shared.

When they left the clinic, the sun had already dipped low in the sky, and a gentle breeze carried the scent of earth, hay, and the faint smell of leather from saddles, mixing with the occasional hint of coal smoke. Paul kept a hand on Elsie's back as they walked.

Elsie looked at him. "You think he'll be alright here?"

"I think he will. He's picked up all sorts of crafts on the trail—we all do. He'll find something to spend his days on."

"I'm glad. He deserves the peace."

"That he does." Paul glanced at her, seeing the softness in her eyes as she looked around the town. "We could stay here too, you know."

"What about your ranch?"

"I don't care about it as long as I'm with you."

"Well, I'd like to see it first." She looked up at him, a small smile tugging at her lips. "We might just find our peace there."

The words warmed Paul more than he expected. There was something about the idea of peace with Elsie that made everything else seem manageable, even the uncertainties of the future. He found himself smiling back at her, his chest filled with something he could only describe as hope.

Back at the boarding house, the warmth of the fire in the main room welcomed them.

Paul sat down heavily on a sofa, and Elsie curled up beside him, her head resting on his shoulder. They sat and watched the flames dance for a while. The fire pulled them into a trance, each crackle and pop a reminder of how far they'd come and how much they had overcome.

"Oh, I have something for you." Elsie's voice was barely above a whisper. She pulled a small slip of paper from her pocket and handed it to Paul.

"A telegram?" Paul frowned as he took it from her and unfolded it.

The message was short, congratulating Paul and Elsie on a successful cattle drive and their new marriage. How Aldo had found out that Elsie was a woman or that they'd gotten married, the telegram didn't say. Paul suspected that Aldo's buyer had hung around town long enough to see the shooting and then looked into the parties that had participated in it.

"Well, can't say I expected that." Paul folded the paper. "Never took the old man for the sentimental type."

Elsie chuckled. "Seems like he's finally taking it easy too."

Paul nodded, and they shared a quiet moment, the warmth of the fire wrapping around them both. Paul leaned over and pressed a soft kiss to the top of Elsie's head. She sighed contentedly, sinking further into his side.

Paul shifted slightly and wrapped his arm around her more securely, feeling her warmth against him. The soft crackle of the fire and the occasional pop of the wood echoed the steady beat of his heart.

Elsie lifted her head, her eyes meeting his with a gentle intensity. There was something unspoken in her gaze— gratitude, love, and the quiet relief of simply being together after everything they had endured.

Paul brushed a strand of hair away from her face, his fingers lingering for a moment on her cheek. "I'm not sure I deserve all this."

"You deserve everything, Paul." She leaned in closer, her lips brushing his, a feather-light kiss that deepened as they both surrendered to the moment. It was tender, slow—an affirmation of all the unspoken promises between them. When they pulled back, Elsie rested her forehead against his.

"We've come so far," she whispered, her breath warm against his lips. "And we've still got so much more to discover."

Paul nodded, his heart swelling with emotion he couldn't quite name—love, hope, and something that felt a lot like belonging. He held her tighter, pressing his lips to her forehead once more.

"As long as we're together," he said, "that's all that matters."

The fire flickered, casting dancing shadows around the room, and for the first time in years, Paul allowed himself to let go of the past. To imagine a future full of warmth, love, and the woman beside him. The world outside could wait. Here, with Elsie in his arms and the firelight glowing around them, everything felt right.

"Two days ago, I never thought we'd be here," Paul murmured.

"Neither did I," Elsie whispered back.

But here they were. Together.

Chapter Twenty-Nine

Paul's Ranch

The Texas sun hung low in the sky, bathing the landscape in a deep amber glow as Paul guided Spirit down the winding trail that led to his ranch. His heart thudded harder than he cared to admit. He'd pictured this homecoming countless times, but today was different—today, he wasn't alone.

Beside him, Elsie rode with a quiet determination, her eyes wide as she took it all in. The land was still scarred from the years of neglect—broken fences, fields choked with weeds, the house itself standing like a lone sentinel—but it was his.

Well, now, it was *theirs.*

As they crested the final hill, the ranch came into full view. Paul swallowed hard. The place was a shadow of what it once had been. His father had built it with his own hands, and after the war, Paul had tried to piece it back together. But no matter how much he worked, it had never really felt like home again. Not after everything that had happened.

He tightened his grip on the reins, nerves fluttering in his chest. Would Elsie see it the same way Katherine had—a lost cause, not worth her time?

He risked a glance at her, his heart hammering with a mixture of hope and dread.

To his surprise, Elsie's eyes were shining. She broke into a grin, her face lighting up as she dismounted quickly, her feet hitting the dusty earth. She began to walk forward, her gaze roving over the land, taking in every corner, every broken piece of it. She looked excited, pointing toward the old barn with its sagging roof, and the fields that stretched out beyond.

"Look, Paul!" she called, her voice filled with enthusiasm. "We could fix that roof, maybe put in a new door for the barn—and imagine how the fields could look with a proper fence line! We could grow crops here again, maybe get a good vegetable garden going—and those pastures could be perfect for grazing if we—"

She stopped. Paul hadn't moved; he was still sitting atop his horse, staring at her, his face blank.

Her smile faded, and she tucked a loose curl behind her ear. "I... I mean, it's your home—I shouldn't... It's not my place to decide..."

Paul swung himself down from the saddle, his boots thudding against the ground as he crossed the short distance between them. He took her hands gently in his, lifting her chin so she'd look at him.

"No, Elsie," he said, his voice low but sure. "It's *our* home."

Her eyes widened. "But—"

"I'm sorry." He pulled her into his arms, wrapping her tight against his chest. "I was just stunned by how lucky I am to have you. All of this is ours to fix and ours to build—*together.*"

She let out a breath, one that sounded like a mix of laughter and relief, and hugged him back fiercely. Paul rested his chin on top of her head, holding her close, feeling the warmth of her body against his. He'd never thought he'd find someone who saw what he did when he looked at this place. Someone who could see past the broken boards and empty fields and imagine something beautiful. Someone who believed in the potential it still held.

Someone who believed in him.

They stood like that for a long moment, wrapped in each other, until Elsie pulled back slightly, her cheeks flushed with emotion.

"Alright, then," she said, her voice light and teasing. "Let's get to it, partner."

Paul smiled, his heart swelling with love for this woman, who'd come into his life and changed everything. He turned, keeping an arm around her as they walked toward the house. The cabin loomed large, its logs darkened with age, the front door hanging slightly off its hinges.

Paul pushed it open, the familiar creak of wood echoing in the stillness.

Inside, the cabin was much as he'd left it—sparse, a table pushed to one side, a couple of chairs, and the fireplace he'd repaired so many times it felt like an old friend. The light filtered in through the windows, dust motes swirling in the sunbeams. He glanced over at Elsie, watching her expression as she took it all in. She wandered through the room, her fingers trailing along the rough wood of the table, her eyes lingering on the hearth.

"It's bigger than I expected." She turned back to Paul, her cheeks reddening a bit. "Big enough for... for children someday, I think."

Paul's breath caught in his chest.

Children. He hadn't let himself think about that—not since the war, and certainly not since Katherine had left. The idea of a family had seemed so far out of reach, something for other men, men who weren't scarred by loss and violence. But now, standing here with Elsie, seeing the hope in her eyes, he felt something warm bloom in his chest. Children. A future.

He stepped closer, cupping her cheek in his hand, his thumb brushing lightly against her skin. "You think so?"

She nodded, her eyes shining with tears. "I do."

Paul swallowed hard, a lump forming in his throat. He pulled her into a kiss, gentle at first, then deeper, pouring everything he felt into that moment—love, hope, fear, and the promise of a life they could build together. When they broke apart, he rested his forehead against hers, his eyes closed.

"Then we'll make this place a real home. For us. For whatever comes next."

Elsie smiled. "We'll make it grand, Paul. You'll see."

They spent the rest of the day walking the land, talking about their plans. Paul found himself smiling more than he had in years, listening as Elsie spoke of gardens and livestock, of what they could grow and build together. Her excitement was infectious, and as he watched her move across the fields, the golden strands of her hair catching the sunlight, he felt something inside him settle.

This was right. This was what he'd been searching for, even when he hadn't known it.

As the sun disappeared below the horizon, they returned to the cabin, their arms full of firewood. Paul stacked the logs by the hearth while Elsie lit a lamp, its soft glow filling the room. They sat together in front of the fire, their legs touching, the warmth of the flames wrapping around them like a blanket.

"Tell me more about your plans for the cattle," Elsie said, leaning against his shoulder.

Paul wrapped an arm around her, his fingers brushing against her arm. "I was thinking we could start small," he said. "Maybe ten, fifteen head to begin with. Build up the herd as we go. There's still good grazing land nearby, and the railroad's made it easier to move them when the time comes. I'd like to work with the tribes in the Oklahoma territory too—bring some cattle to Hattak and his people next spring. We could visit, see how they're doing."

Elsie lifted her head, her eyes brightening. "Hattak! I'd love that. Maybe they'd even have some advice for us. About the land, the livestock."

Paul nodded, a smile tugging at his lips. "I reckon they would. Hattak's got a good head on his shoulders. It'd be good to see him settled. He should have himself a wife now."

Elsie laughed, the sound warm and full of life. "Oh, that's wonderful! I can't wait to meet her." She looked at Paul, her gaze softening. "It sounds like a good plan, Paul. A real future."

Paul pressed a kiss to her forehead, his heart full. "Yeah," he said softly. "A real future."

Paul allowed himself to dream of the days ahead. There would be hard work, no doubt. There would be struggles and setbacks. But with Elsie by his side, he knew they could handle whatever came. She was his partner, his equal—someone who could teach him as much as he could teach her, someone who believed in him, and in the life they could build together.

And as they sat there, the fire crackling in the hearth, Paul felt peace. He looked around the cabin, at the walls that had once felt empty, at the woman beside him who'd filled his life with light, and he knew. This was home.

Finally, truly, it was home.

Epilogue

En route to Hattak's village

The sun hung low in the sky, casting long shadows across the Oklahoma plains as Paul rode beside Elsie, their horses plodding steadily forward. The warm breeze carried the scent of wild grasses and stirred the leaves of the scattered oaks dotting the landscape. Elsie sat tall in the saddle beside him, her hand resting instinctively on her stomach every now and then, her gaze fixed on the horizon ahead where Hattak and his wife Achukma Ahoyyo would be meeting them.

Elsie was three months pregnant, and despite Paul's protests, she'd insisted on coming along for this last cattle drive.

Paul glanced sideways at her, feeling a familiar mix of love and worry. "You should be resting, not traipsing across the plains," he muttered.

Elsie gave him a quick smile, her eyes flashing. "You worry too much," she said lightly, brushing off his concern as she had so many times before. "I'm fine, and you know it."

Paul huffed, his expression somewhere between a grin and a grimace. Before he could argue further, a flicker of movement drew his attention.

Hattak and Achukma Ahoyyo emerged from the line of trees up ahead, their figures silhouetted against the late afternoon sky. Hattak raised his hand in greeting, a broad smile splitting his face as he and Achukma rode forward to meet them.

Paul could see the genuine joy in Hattak's expression, and he couldn't help but smile as well, even if he still had half a mind to grumble about Elsie coming along. As they reached each other, Hattak's laughter boomed out, his eyes twinkling as he took in Elsie's determined expression and Paul's disapproving look.

"Paul, your woman is strong," Hattak said, clapping Paul on the shoulder. "It's good she's here, working. The baby will be strong too—just like his mother!"

Paul gave a resigned smile, shaking his head. "I suppose there's no stopping her. She's always been stubborn."

Elsie rolled her eyes and shot Paul a look before smiling warmly at Achukma. The two women exchanged pleasantries, their voices brightening the dusty landscape around them. Achukma reached across to clasp Elsie's hand, and before long, the two were riding side by side, chatting animatedly as they headed toward the Choctaw village.

Paul let them move ahead, his gaze lingering on Elsie for a moment longer, affection and pride swelling in his chest. He turned to Hattak, who was now guiding his horse beside his, and together, they fell into a comfortable rhythm, driving the fifty head of cattle along the trail.

The clinking of the cattle bells and the steady thud of hooves created a soothing backdrop, allowing the men to talk without hurry. They spoke of the small things first—cattle prices, the changing seasons—but soon the conversation turned heavier, as it often did these days.

"I fear we will lose more of our land soon," Hattak said, his voice tinged with frustration. He gestured toward the horizon, where the faint lines of the railroad cut across the earth. "The railroad spreads, and more tribes are selling their lands to the government. I don't know how much longer we can hold out."

Paul nodded, his jaw tightening. "It's a damn shame," he said quietly. "The land's changing faster than I can keep up with. Used to be we could ride for days and never see a soul. Now it's all fences, tracks, and towns springing up like weeds." He paused, glancing toward Elsie and Achukma. "That's how I met her, you know. Out in the wild, when it was still untamed."

Hattak smiled gently, his eyes following Paul's gaze. "And now, you're happy to leave it all behind?"

Paul considered the question, letting the silence stretch out between them. He watched Elsie's silhouette, the way she threw her head back when she laughed, the sunlight catching in her hair. He nodded slowly. "Yeah," he said, his voice thoughtful. "I think I am. I'm ready for something different. It's been a long time coming, but I don't need the wild anymore. I've got what I need right here."

Hattak's grin broadened, and he gave Paul a knowing nod. "That is good, brother. We all need to find peace, in our own way."

Paul smiled, but a heaviness lingered. "Elsie still has her bad nights," he admitted after a pause. "She dreams about her past, the horrors that Jon put her through. But now, with the baby coming, it feels like a fresh start for both of us." He looked over at Hattak, his expression earnest. "It's strange, Hattak. For the first time, I think I understand what home really means."

Hattak nodded, his expression serious. "A new family, a new home. It is a good beginning."

Paul sighed, his gaze turning westward, his thoughts drifting. "I heard Layton's still lurking about. Apparently, he's gathered a gang of his own, and marshals are trying to hunt 'em down." He shrugged. "Still, Elsie's insisting that Layton wants nothing to do with us, and I believe her. He certainly hasn't shown his face at our ranch yet."

Hattak's brow furrowed slightly. "That kind of life is a dark path," he said quietly. "Do you think they'll come this way?"

Paul shook his head. "No. I don't think he'll come for Elsie. After all, he saved her life, in a way. They're moving west, and we're staying out of it. I've had enough of the guns, the running, the danger. I want something different for us. For her. For the baby."

Hattak looked at him thoughtfully. "You have had your share of loss and violence, Paul. It is right to want peace. To protect your family."

Paul nodded, his gaze softening as he watched Elsie up ahead. "It's time to focus on happiness. We've had enough drama, enough loss. This is our last cattle drive. After this, we'll be working with the railroad—keeping inventory, liaising with merchants. It'll be steady, safe work."

Hattak smiled. "And that makes you happy?"

"More than I ever thought possible," Paul said, his voice low but full of conviction.

They rode on in silence for a while, the sounds of the cattle and the creaking of leather saddles filling the space between them. The Oklahoma plains rolled out endlessly around them, the grasses swaying gently in the breeze.

Paul let the quiet settle, taking in the vastness of it all, the openness that had once been his lifeline. He thought of all the years he'd spent alone, moving from one place to the next, always looking for something he couldn't name. And now, here he was, with a woman he loved, a child on the way, and a future that felt solid and real.

As they approached the Choctaw village, the sight of the small cluster of homes, the smoke from cooking fires curling into the sky, and the sound of children laughing reached them. Elsie and Achukma had already dismounted, their laughter echoing back toward Paul and Hattak. Paul watched Elsie, her hands moving as she spoke, her smile wide and bright, and he felt that warmth in his chest again—that undeniable sense of belonging.

Hattak glanced at him, a gentle smile tugging at his lips. "You have found your place, Paul. That is a rare thing."

Paul met his friend's eyes, his own smile growing. "Yeah," he said softly. "I guess I have."

As they herded the cattle into the makeshift pen near the village, Paul found himself thinking about what lay ahead. There was a lot of work to be done, but it was work he looked forward to. A future filled with honest labor, laughter, and love. The railroad, the new baby, the ranch—it was all part of the life he wanted to build.

Maybe one day, he'd tell his child about these times—the cattle drives, the wide-open plains, and the adventures that had brought him and Elsie together. But more than that, he wanted his child to know about the love that had carried them through it all, the hope that had kept them going, even when things seemed darkest.

As the sun crept toward the horizon, painting the sky in shades of red and orange, Paul and Elsie stood side by side, watching the cattle settle, the village coming to life around them. Elsie slipped her hand into his, her fingers lacing with his, and Paul turned to look at her, his heart full.

"This is it," he said quietly. "Our new beginning."

Elsie smiled, her eyes soft, her free hand resting on her stomach. "Yes, it is," she whispered, "and I wouldn't have it any other way."

Paul pulled her close, pressing a kiss to her temple, his eyes closing as he savored the moment. The future was waiting for them, full of hope, promise, and the kind of love that could heal even the deepest wounds.

For the first time, Paul felt truly ready for it. And he knew that, with Elsie by his side, there was nothing they couldn't face. Together, they would build their home, raise their family, and find the happiness they had both fought so hard to earn.

THE END

Also by Zachary McCrae

Thank you for reading **"The Trail Boss "**!

If you liked this book, you can also check out **my full Amazon Book Catalogue at:**
https://go.zacharymccrae.com/bc-authorpage

Thank you!

Printed in Great Britain
by Amazon